"I'm not in the habit of behaving like this."

Both Luke's hands were now cupping Melanie's face, his thumbs stroking her skin, soothing her jangling nerves, calming her panic, the slow sound of his voice almost mesmeric.

Even so she still managed to tell him shakily, "That wasn't the impression I got the first time we met."

"That was different," he told her huskily. "Then it was just a game."

It took her a long time and a lot of courage to ask, "And now?"

His thumbs were still caressing her skin, but now the sensation wasn't soothing—it was erotic, dangerous, compelling.

"And now it isn't a game anymore," he told her seriously. "Not for me."

PENNY JORDAN was constantly in trouble in school because of her inability to stop daydreaming—especially during French lessons. In her teens, she was an avid romance reader, although it didn't occur to her to try writing one herself until she was older. "My first half-dozen attempts ended up ingloriously," she remembers, "but I persevered, and one manuscript was finished." She plucked up the courage to send it to a publisher, convinced her book would be rejected. It wasn't, and the rest is history! Penny is married and lives in Cheshire.

Penny Jordan's striking mainstream novel *Power Play* quickly became a *New York Times* bestseller. She followed that success with *Silver*, a story of ambition, passion and intrigue, and *The Hidden Years*, a novel that lays bare the choices all women face in their search for love.

Watch for Penny's latest blockbuster, *Lingering Shadows*, available in August.

Books by Penny Jordan

PENNY JORDAN

A Time To Dream

Harlequin Books

TORONTO • NEW YORK • LONDON
AMSTERDAM • PARIS • SYDNEY • HAMBURG
STOCKHOLM • ATHENS • TOKYO • MILAN
MADRID • WARSAW • BUDAPEST • AUCKLAND

Harlequin Presents first edition February 1993
ISBN 0-373-11529-6

Original hardcover edition published in 1991
by Mills & Boon Limited

A TIME TO DREAM

CHAPTER ONE

WHEN the telephone started to ring, Melanie was poised precariously on the narrow platform of a pair of heavy wooden stepladders. The tip of her tongue was curled determinedly between her lips as she concentrated on trying to successfully hang the all-important, first piece of wallpaper on walls which fell woefully short of being anything remotely like flat and straight.

Firmly ignoring the insistent clamour of the phone, she carefully pressed the pasted paper to the wall, but already her concentration was wavering.

The trouble was that—much as she had looked forward to the isolation of these next few months, telling herself that a spring and summer spent in the peaceful depths of the country, gently and leisurely bringing into reasonable decorative order the cottage she had been so unexpectedly left; much as she knew she needed this period of valuable recuperation to recover not just from a very nasty bout of flu, but also from the anguish of discovering that Paul had not loved her after all, and had simply been amusing himself with her while all the time intending to marry Sarah Jefferies and thus amalgamate the two businesses owned and run by their respective fathers—she was still beginning to feel rather alone.

She had been warned about Paul, of course. The older, wiser eyes of Louise Jenkins, her boss and the head of Carmichael's PR department, had seen what was happening and had gently warned her not to place too much reliance on Paul and the attention he was paying her.

Fortunately her pride had probably been more hurt than her heart, especially when she had discovered that the very weekend she had firmly refused to go away with Paul he had then spent with Sarah.

When Louise had gently and sorrowfully broken this news to her, warning her of the impending engagement, she had hidden the pain she felt and had tossed her head defiantly, stating that she did not care, and that Paul Carmichael meant nothing to her.

She was very wise, Louise had remarked calmly, because she suspected that Paul was too shallow, too vain and self-obsessed to make any woman truly happy, and that, once she was married to him and her father's business empire was secured for Carmichael's, Sarah would find that Paul's present pseudo-adoration of her would very quickly turn to indifference.

Melanie had listened and mechanically agreed with Louise's pronouncement, but inside the shock of what she had learned was making her feel sick and desperately unhappy.

Now Melanie was only glad that the flu which had then struck her down had not manifested itself until after the engagement party, which all the staff had been commanded to attend, and that, even though she had felt as though she were being wrenched apart inside, she had managed to put in an appearance at the table reserved for her colleagues, a bright false smile pinned to her face as she joined in the celebrations.

It didn't matter how much she told herself that she had had a lucky escape; that it was plain that Paul had never intended her to be anything other than a brief diversion in his life: the pain of discovering how poor her judgement had been, how foolish her heart, was not easy to dismiss.

And then had come the extraordinary letter from a hitherto unknown firm of solicitors, informing her that she was the sole beneficiary under the will of a certain John William Burrows, who had left her not only the entire contents of his bank account, which amounted to some fifty thousand pounds, but also a comfortably sized but very dilapidated cottage, together with its large overgrown garden and several acres of land on the outskirts of a tiny Cheshire village.

She should, the solicitors informed her when she presented herself at their offices, have no difficulty in selling the property; a course which they had recommended since Mr Burrows had been rather eccentric in the latter years of his life and the property had become extremely run-down.

'Were there no blood relatives, no family to whom Mr Burrows could have left his estate?' Melanie had asked anxiously, totally unable to understand why her unknown benefactor had chosen to leave everything to her.

'Only one,' she had been informed. 'A second cousin with whom Mr Burrows had not apparently seen eye to eye.'

When she had asked with further anxiety if the estate ought not more properly have gone to this man, the solicitor had patiently advised her that Mr Burrows had been free to dispose of his assets to whomever he chose and that *he* had chosen her.

His cousin, moreover, was a successful and wealthy businessman to whom, or so the solicitor seemed to imply, the inheritance of such a paltry sum as fifty thousand pounds and a very run-down property, would be more of a nuisance than an advantage.

If it had not been for the fact that she had been feeling so run down herself, so depressed with life in general and her own circumstances in particular, if the bright spring sunshine had not so deplorably highlighted the deficiencies of her small Manchester bedsit ... if she had not been overwhelmed by a sharp surge of curiosity about not merely the cottage but John Burrows himself, she suspected that she would have accepted the solicitor's advice and instructed them to sell the house and land immediately.

It had been Louise who had persuaded her that the cottage was almost heaven sent and that six months or so spent living in the country was just what she needed right now.

'But I don't know anything about living in the country,' she had protested, and Louise had laughed at her, pointing out that Cheshire was hardly the deepest South American jungle.

'If you like, Simon and I will drive you out there this weekend and you can take a look at the place.'

Since Simon, Louise's husband, was a qualified surveyor and would be able to tell her just how dilapidated the property actually was, Melanie had gratefully accepted this suggestion.

Which was how she now came to be perched so precariously on top of this ladder, trying desperately to follow Louise's and Simon's advice that, since the cottage was basically sound, it would pay her to spend some time and money on redecorating it before putting it up for sale.

'Although if you do decide to sell you must hold on to the land,' Simon had warned her. 'There's some talk of a new motorway extension in the area, which could send the price of any local land soaring.'

The phone had thankfully now stopped ringing, and very gingerly she climbed back down the ladder to survey the results of her handiwork.

When she had explained to the man in the wallpaper shop the condition of the cottage walls, explaining that she wanted to do something to brighten up the dull dinginess, she had been thrilled when he had suggested this pretty floral paper with its soft pinks and blues on a gentle cream background. Since there was no formal pattern to the paper it would not matter so much that the walls were not completely straight, he had explained to her; and the fact that the paper was ready-pasted and needed only to be moistened in the specially provided water-tray would greatly assist her in this her first venture as a wallpaper-hanger.

And then if all else failed he did just happen to have the name and address of an excellent local decorator, he had added with a kind smile, correctly interpreting her uncertain look at what seemed to be a vast amount of rolls of paper.

The trouble was that she had lived so long in rented accommodation in the confines of one tiny cluttered room that she was completely inexperienced in this sort of thing.

Before that her home had been the shabby institutionalised atmosphere of the children's home where she had grown up.

When Melanie was orphaned when just three years old, there had been no one to take her into their charge. As she had grown up and realised how alone in the world she was, she had learned to cover the loneliness and aching sense of loss this brought her with a bright smile and an insouciant air of cheerfulness, while inwardly giving in to the compulsion to daydream on what her life might have been if her parents had not been killed in that car crash.

Perhaps it had been that inner loneliness, that need she had always tried to keep so firmly under control which had made her so susceptible to Paul's false declaration of love.

Louise had been right about one thing. Living here in this cottage was giving her a new perspective on life.

Always fiercely independent, fiercely determined not to rely on anyone for anything, she was beginning to discover that needing the companionship, the friendship of others was not perhaps a weakness after all, but simply an acceptable fact of being human.

She had been surprised to discover how curious people were about her, and how ready they were to express that curiosity. The cottage was situated almost two miles outside the village, but already Melanie had had several callers, no doubt curious to see the young woman to whom old Mr Burrows had left his property.

Melanie still had no idea why on earth John Burrows had left his estate to her, and the solicitors had been as baffled as she was herself.

She frowned, worried as she studied her wallpaper, wondering if it was straight enough.

She wasn't a very tall girl, barely five feet three with fine delicate bones that made her look far more fragile than she actually was. Her debilitating attack of flu had left her looking more finely drawn than ever, leaving shadows beneath her dark blue eyes and a listlessness to her normally energetic way of moving.

Today her long dark hair was tied back off her face and plaited, making her look much younger than her twenty-four years.

Twenty-four. Paul had laughed at her when she had turned down his suggestion that they spend the weekend together. She couldn't possibly still be a virgin, he had mocked her. Not at her age and with her background.

That had hurt her; as though somehow the fact that she had no family to support and protect her meant that she must somehow be promiscuous. She had immediately denied such a suggestion, ignoring the unkind way he was laughing at her.

As a child she had loved reading; had found in her books an escape from the loneliness of her life, and perhaps it was because she had absorbed so many fairy-tales that she had clung so tenaciously during her late teens to the fantasy that one day she would meet someone; that they would fall in love and that not until that happened would she have any desire for the kind of sexual intimacy that seemed so casually taken for granted by others.

Perhaps Paul *was* right and she *was* being naïve and idiotic; perhaps it was true that the majority of men *would* deplore and mock her inexperience; perhaps it was also true that at her age she ought to finally be abandoning her ridiculous notions of falling in love and living happily ever after.

Certainly, now that her eyes had been opened to Paul's true character, she would not want to change places with Sarah.

Very carefully she cut the next strip of wallpaper, equally carefully rolling it up and placing it in the water-filled tray.

It had been Louise who had suggested that she tried her hand at doing some of her own decorating, taking Melanie home with her to show her what she and Simon had achieved in their own elegant detached house.

Some ten years her senior, Louise was proving to be a good friend, the first real friend she had ever had. She and Simon had been very kind to her and they were the only people she had ever admitted into her life and her trust.

Quite why, when she was eighteen years old, she had decided to take a course of driving lessons and ultimately her driving test she had never really known, but now she was thoroughly glad she had done so. Although Melanie was reluctant at first to touch any of her savings, Louise and Simon had firmly told her that when living in such an isolated area a car was an absolute necessity, and then when she had seen the fire-engine red VW Beetle she had fallen so immediately in love with it that Louise had chided her teasingly about being a salesman's dream.

She did not intend to touch a penny of her inheritance—she had other plans for that!

Wealth, luxuries, life in what was popularly termed 'the fast lane'—these had no appeal whatsoever for Melanie, but what she *had* always secretly hankered for was a home of her own, preferably in a country setting.

Of course in her daydreams this home was peopled with the family she had never had, but perhaps that was why she had given in so easily to Louise's urgings that she move into the cottage if only for a little while.

Perhaps there had also been another reason; perhaps she had hoped that in living in the cottage she might somehow discover more about her unknown benefactor.

Melanie didn't know very much about men, as the lamentable way in which she had almost fallen for Paul's deceit had shown. She had no idea why a man, a total stranger, should choose to make her the beneficiary of his will. The solicitors had suggested that perhaps there was a blood connection, but she had shaken her head, knowing already that she had no blood relatives whatsoever.

Perhaps, then, he had known her parents. Again she had shaken her head, forced to admit that she had no idea whether or not this might have been the case, but privately she doubted it. If he had, surely he would have come forward to make himself known to her while he was still alive.

Apart from his cousin, it seemed that John Burrows had had no other family. He had lived in the area all his life and so had his family before him, although in the latter years of his life he had apparently become something of a recluse.

Carefully Melanie mounted the ladder again, gingerly carrying the second piece of wallpaper.

This proved harder to stick on to the wall than the first piece. Even harder was trying to align the edges of the two pieces so that the random pattern matched. The damp paper tore, causing her to make a small verbal protest at her own lack of skill as she hastily tried to stop the paper ripping even further.

Perhaps if she hadn't been concentrating so hard on what she was doing it would not have been such a shock when the bedroom door opened abruptly and a totally unfamiliar male voice called out cheerfully, 'Sorry to barge in like this. I tried ringing the bell but couldn't get any response and, since your back door was open...'

Automatically Melanie let go of the sticky paper and turned round, forgetting her precarious position on top of the ladder.

The man's reactions were fast. As the ladder started to topple and she with it, he seemed to virtually leap forward across the room, grabbing her around the waist and swinging her free of the heavy ladders just as they crashed down on to the floor.

It must be the shock of both his totally unexpected appearance and nearly having a painful fall that was making her feel so weak, she decided shakily, unable to do a thing other than simply cling to the hard muscles of his arms while he held her firmly suspended quite some distance from the floor, his black-lashed grey eyes subjecting her to a very thorough and slow appraisal.

As the colour rose up under her skin, her body language betraying immediately that she was both unused to and not entirely comfortable with such intimacy, his expression changed, a tiny frown appearing between his dark eyebrows as he studied her again.

What was it about her that was bringing that almost irritated frown to those otherwise rather carefully blank grey eyes? Melanie wondered when she found the courage to shyly look into them.

He was still holding on to her, as effortlessly as though she were a small child, she realised rather indignantly as she struggled uncomfortably within his grasp, trying to remind him that he was still holding her some dozen or more inches off the floor.

When this gave no response, she demanded rather breathlessly, 'Could you please put me down?'

He had stopped looking at her, thankfully, and seemed to be studying the wall behind her with a rather arrested and bemused look on his face. The wall she had just been papering, she realised defensively; but now he looked at her again, and her whole body seemed to receive a shocking jolt of sensation that made her feel literally as though her bones had turned to fluid and that if he put her down now she would simply dissolve into a small heap at his feet.

The trouble was that she wasn't used to being so physically close to a man; and certainly not a man like this one. He might not be handsome in the way that Paul had been. Paul, with his blond good looks, his carefully groomed hair, his hard, compelling bone-structure and his equally hard muscles; but this man had something about him, something which she dimly recognised was far more potent and dangerously male than Paul's rather effeminate and weak good looks.

'Not yet, I think,' the stranger told her easily. 'First I demand my forfeit...'

'Your forfeit...' Melanie was unaware of saying the words aloud in a stupefied almost drugged voice until he smiled at her. She had often read of smiles being described as wolfish, but this was the first time she had ever seen one. It made her skin go cold and then hot, and a tiny, forbidden pulse of excitement beat into life deep within her body; a sensation so unfamiliar and shocking that she could only stare at him with her bewilderment openly betrayed in her eyes.

His own narrowed fractionally, their blankness suddenly sharpening into an expression that made her heart jump frantically, but thankfully he seemed to mistake the cause of her shock because he explained patiently as though speaking to a child, 'Yes, the forfeit you owe me for so speedily saving you from misfortune. That's the way it goes in all the best fairy-tales, isn't it?'

Her heart jumped again. She averted her head, but couldn't resist giving him a nervous sideways look. She licked her lips anxiously. He had said that almost as though he *knew* her; as though he knew of her childhood absorption and belief in such things.

But she wasn't a child any more. She was a twenty-four-year-old woman, and he was a strange man who had no right to walk into her home even if she *had* misguidedly left the back door open.

However, before she could say as much he was speaking again, his voice soft, mesmeric almost. 'You have such a warm, irresistible mouth that there's really only one forfeit I can ask you for, isn't there? A mouth like yours was surely fashioned deliberately to entice a man's kisses.'

Her head was whirling. What on earth was happening to her? Things like this simply did not take place. Men such as this one simply did not walk into her life and demand forfeits from her... kisses... And as for what he had said about her mouth...

Unconsciously she traced its shape with her tongue tip, her eyes unwittingly darkening in reaction to the potency of what he had whispered to her, her naïvety and lack of experience so openly obvious that for a moment he hesitated.

What if his assumptions should be wrong? She looked so fragile...so lost...so vulnerable somehow; and then he reminded himself that he could not afford to make mistakes or allowances; that he had come here for one express purpose; that he... He tensed as she focused on him, her eyes so dark that they looked almost purple, so dilated that...

He felt his own heartbeat quicken, his body tensing in reaction to the scent and the warmth of her...the womanliness... Because she *was* a woman, despite the fragility of her body and the innocence in her eyes.

He lowered his head, sternly reminding himself why he was doing this.

Held fast in his arms, Melanie quivered nervously. He *was* going to kiss her; she knew it. She also knew she ought to stop him, but how could she? What was her puny strength against the hard bulk of his body?

The grey glance still held her own, inducing an almost trance-like state of stillness within her body.

She felt the warmth of his breath caress her cheek, and a rush of goose-pimples raced down her body.

She quivered once as his mouth touched hers, her body stiffening as her mind summoned all its feminine defences, desperately sensing an enemy more dangerous than any it had yet known, but her body was deaf to all the warnings of her brain.

He kissed her slowly and lingeringly, bemusing her so thoroughly that she wasn't even aware of him gradually lowering her so that her feet could once more touch the floor, thus freeing his hands to cup her face and her arms to instinctively and betrayingly creep round his neck, her heart pounding suffocatingly, as his tongue tip stroked her trembling lips. The hand cupping her jaw held her still beneath his sensual assault, while its partner slid down her back, firmly moulding her against body.

Paul had kissed her. Several times and very passionately, or so she had thought, and there had been other kisses before that, but none like this; and for all the fact that there was none of the urgency, the greed of Paul's kisses in this man's almost detached possession of her mouth, she was still aware of a reaction within herself that was far, far more intense and dangerous that any emotion Paul had ever made her feel.

In fact, when he eventually started to release her mouth, her lips actually seemed to cling to his. And she knew that he was aware of it too because he made a sound beneath his breath which might have been irritation or which might have been amusement.

Thankfully whatever it was it brought her sharply back to reality in time to remove her arms from around his neck before he had to forcibly do it for her. However, when he stepped back from her, to her consternation she discovered that her body seemed to actively miss the hard pressure of his.

While she was still trying to come to terms with what had happened he stepped past her to examine her wallpapering, commenting almost brusquely,

'You know, these ladders aren't really safe. Some lightweight aluminium ones would be far better. Think what could have happened if you *had* fallen and I hadn't been here to catch you.'

If he hadn't been there she wouldn't have fallen off the ladders in the first place, Melanie told herself sturdily. Now that he wasn't touching her any more she was rapidly returning to sanity, to the awareness that he was a stranger who had invaded the privacy of her home, uninvited, and that, for all that her feminine awareness of him urged her to think differently, he could be dangerous.

'Umm...' he added, moving closer to the wall on which she was working. 'It looks to me as though you could do with a plumb-line!'

'A plumb-line?' She stared at him.

'Mm. If you've got a piece of string and some chalk I'll show you what I mean.'

He turned round then and smiled at her, a warm gentle smile that made her heart turn over.

'I am sorry,' he apologised. 'You must be wondering who on earth I am and what I'm doing barging in on you like this. I've just moved into the cottage at the bottom of the lane, only to discover that none of the services seem to have been switched on. I was hoping I could use your phone to make a couple of calls. My name's Luke, by the way.'

'Luke,' Melanie repeated, automatically reaching out to shake the hand he had extended to her.

His grip was firm without being painful, the palm of his hand slightly callused as though he worked outside, and yet, for all the casualness of his jeans and shirt, there was an air about him which suggested that he was a man used more to giving orders than following them. But then, what did she know about men? Melanie derided herself a little forlornly.

'Luke?' she queried a little more firmly, determined to let him know that she wasn't a complete fool.

'Luke Chalmers,' he told her easily, adding softly, 'I hope you aren't too angry with me for taking advantage of the opportunity that fate so generously gave me.'

Angry! Her heart skipped a beat. Anger wasn't exactly how she would describe her confused and chaotic emotions, but from somewhere she found the presence of mind to respond drily, 'Do you make a habit of going round demanding forfeits from women you don't know?'

'Only when they're as beautiful and tempting as you,' he told her gravely. 'And that, fortunately, is very rare. So rare in fact that I've never known it to happen before.'

Her heart was thumping frantically again. She felt as though she was suddenly caught up in a new game—a game that was both wildly exciting and frighteningly dangerous.

'You wanted to use the phone,' she reminded him breathlessly. 'It's downstairs. I'll show you.'

As she walked past him he caught hold of her arm, his fingers sliding almost caressingly over the softness of its inner flesh so that she quivered. His fingers encircled her wrist, holding her in bondage while his free hand moved up to her face.

He wasn't going to kiss her again was he? He wasn't going to repeat that mind-blowing, devastating caress? No, he wasn't, it seemed. He reached out and removed something from her face, causing her to gasp a little as she felt a sharp sting of pain. She looked at him in surprise as he held a small snippet of her wallpaper between his fingers.

'I believe that in the eighteenth century ladies used to stick false beauty-spots to their faces in order to draw attention to their eyes and mouth, but this is the first time I've ever seen wallpaper being used for the same purpose.

'What a pity it was so close to your cheekbone and not your mouth,' he added sultrily, 'otherwise I might have been tempted to demand another forfeit.'

Melanie thought of all the sensible and authoritative things she ought to have said in response to this outrageous piece of male flirtation, but oddly all she could do was to gaze mutely at him, while inside she prayed desperately that he wouldn't read into her silence the compliant eagerness of her body that he should adopt just such a course.

What on earth was happening to her? After Paul she had surely learned her lesson; had surely realised that it was idiotic to trust men so quickly, that it was dangerous to continue to believe in her childhood dreams and fantasies of finding love and living happily ever after.

'The phone,' she reminded him weakly. 'It's downstairs.'

'Ah, yes, the phone,' he agreed gravely. So gravely that she half suspected that he might be laughing at her. The thought made her face sting with embarrassed colour. Well, if he *was* she surely deserved it, allowing him to take advantage of her like that…allowing him to kiss her…to…to what?

Her bruised heart ached in panicky reaction to her susceptibility to him, reminding her of her vulnerability...reminding her of the close escape she had had from Paul's deceit.

The telephone was in the sitting-room. She escorted him to it and then left him alone, retreating to the kitchen. When he rejoined her she would show him by her dignified silence, by her cool remoteness that whatever might have happened upstairs she was not the kind of woman to be easily influenced by his outrageous brand of flattery and flirtation.

He was a man who was obviously well versed in the ways of her sex, in its vanities and vulnerabilities, and it would be as well to ensure that he was aware right from the start that, close neighbours though they might be, she was simply not interested in the kind of flirtatious, meaningless affair in which he no doubt specialised and that he might just as well save his flattery *and* his kisses for someone more appreciative of them.

However, when he *did* eventually return he was looking so grave that she felt compelled to ask him anxiously, 'Is something wrong?'

'In a sense.' There was no flirtatiousness in his manner now. 'It seems that it's going to be some weeks before the telephone people can put in a phone. Luckily the electricity supply should be on within the next couple of days. Unfortunately, however, my work does mean that I need a telephone.'

'Your work?'

'Yes,' he told her. 'I'm a private detective.'

Melanie stared at him. 'A...a what?'

'A private detective,' he repeated casually. 'I'm working on a case in this area. Naturally I can't disclose any details. I rented the cottage, thinking it would give me a good base from which to work. It's secluded enough to ensure that I don't get too many people wanting to know what I'm doing here. That's the trouble with country areas—people are curious about their neighbours in a way they aren't in the city.'

'Yes, they are, aren't they?' Melanie agreed. She too had discovered that, and it had thrown her a little at first, until she had sensibly realised that behind their curiosity was a very warm neighbourly concern for her well-being.

'You're not local, then?' he asked her almost in surprise.

'Well, no... actually I'm not.'

He paused as though inviting her to go on, and when she did not said softly, 'Then it seems that we have something in common. Two strangers in a foreign land.'

For some reason his words conjured up a warmth within her, a sense of shared intimacy with him that made her react against it, to say primly, 'I should hardly consider Cheshire a foreign land——'

'You think not? The countryside is always a foreign land to a city dweller,' he told her with a grin, adding, before she could respond, 'Look, I've taken up enough of your time. I'd better go.'

To her horror, Melanie discovered that she was almost on the verge of protesting that she didn't want him to leave; that she had to literally bite on the inside of her mouth to stop herself from uttering the betraying words.

Silently she accompanied him to the back door, only able to incline her head in assent when he told her smoothly, 'You really should get that lock seen to, you know. I'm surprised a streetwise city girl like you hasn't had that attended to already.'

The way he said the word 'streetwise' made her tense as though sustaining a blow, as though somehow the words had held an insult, a gibe; and yet when she looked at him the grey eyes were still smiling, the relaxed bulk of the male body carelessly at ease, so that she knew she must have imagined the toughness, the threat which she had momentarily felt lay beneath the words.

Melanie closed the door as soon as he had driven off, bolting it from the inside. He was right about one thing. She *must* get that lock seen to.

Although she went back upstairs, somehow wallpapering had lost its appeal and she discovered that she was wandering restlessly from room to room of her new domain, her thoughts not on the house and all that she had planned to do to it, but on the man who had just left.

She raised her hand to her lips, touching them questingly as though in search of the physical imprint of his. Even without closing her eyes she could recall every detail of those moments in his arms, every nuance of the sensuality of his unexpected kiss.

Stop it, she told herself shakily. Stop it at once. You know how stupid it is to daydream. It's time you grew up...faced reality...accepted life for what it really is.

CHAPTER TWO

EASY enough to say, but far, far harder to do, as Melanie discovered that evening as she tried to concentrate on the gardening books she had borrowed from the local library with the praiseworthy intention of doing what she could to restore order to the wilderness that lay beyond the house.

As she closed her book she was aware of a deep, welling sense of pity and sadness for the man who had willed her this house. How lonely he must have been, and how alone. The house and its environs bore testimony to that solitude; and although it had been a chosen solitude it had not been a happy solitude, she was sure of that. A happy hermit would never have allowed the garden to become so overgrown, or uncared for; a happy hermit would never have turned his back on the comforts his modest wealth could have afforded him to live virtually in the kitchen and his bedroom, as the village gossip had informed her her benefactor had. No; these were the habits of a man whose aloneness, while chosen, was a burden to him, a burden chosen out of bitterness perhaps, out of misery and pain. And yet, why? Why choose to live in the way that he had? Why turn his back on humanity? Why leave his estate to her, a stranger? How had he chosen her—from a list of names which closed eyes and a pin? she wondered unhappily. She had no way of knowing. The solicitors denied any knowledge of how or why he had made his choice, informing her only that it was perfectly legal and his will completely unbreakable.

But what about John Burrows's cousin? she had asked uncertainly. Surely he must have expected to inherit the estate?

Not necessarily, the solicitor had assured her, adding that the two men had quarrelled some years before, and that, besides, the cousin—or, more properly, second cousin—was wealthy enough in his own right not to need to concern himself with his relative's small estate.

Even so, Melanie had not been able to shake off the feeling that somehow a mistake had been made; that she was going to wake up one morning to discover that there *had* been a mistake; that it was another Melanie Foden to whom John Burrows had intended to leave her inheritance.

Although as yet she had not told anyone so, not even Louise, she had decided that at the end of the summer when the cottage was put up for sale whatever monies it brought in she would donate to charity, along with her benefactor's contribution to her substantial bank balance.

The reason why she had not mentioned this plan either to Louise or to the solicitors was that she suspected that they would try to persuade her out of such a decision, but her mind was made up.

Much as she was enjoying her occupation of the cottage, she intended to treat these next few months as a complete break from reality, a voyage of discovery and exploration; a time of healing and rejuvenation, but something apart from her real life to which she fully intended to return once autumn came.

Right now, though, autumn was a long time away and she had a good deal of work to do. Work that involved a careful study of the books piled at her feet and not daydreaming about Luke Chalmers.

Face it, she warned herself as her thoughts traitorously refused to respond to her exhortations. He probably treats every woman the way he did you. It meant nothing... nothing at all. By rights she ought to have stopped him the moment she'd realised he intended to kiss her, instead of standing there like a fool, practically inviting his embrace. And not just inviting it, but enjoying it as well, she acknowledged guiltily as her thoughts and her memories reactivated that wanton throbbing deep within her body which had shocked her so much when she'd been in his arms.

Such feelings were completely unfamiliar to her. Her upbringing in the children's home had never allowed her to give full rein to her burgeoning sexuality, and oddly, although Paul had touched her emotions, kindling the same yearning need for commitment and sharing, for someone with whom she could share her love, which she had experienced so much during her growing years, he had never aroused within her the sensations she had experienced in Luke Chalmers's arms.

Disturbed by the train of her own thoughts, she got up, pacing the sitting-room restlessly.

The cottage was old, its walls irregular and bumpy, its ceilings low and darkened by the heavy beams which supported it.

Like Melanie, it was desperately crying out for love and tenderness, she acknowledged, shivering a little. It worried her constantly, this need she sensed within herself, because she knew how vulnerable it made her, how much in danger she was of mistaking the reactions and responses of others.

Look how she had deceived herself into believing that Paul genuinely cared about her! No wonder that hand in hand with her need had always gone caution and wariness, her mind's defences against the vulnerability of her heart.

She gave another, deeper shiver, wrapping her arms around her slim body as though trying to ward off the danger her mind warned her was waiting for her.

This was ridiculous, she told herself irritably. So Luke Chalmers had kissed her. So what?

So what? She knew quite well what, her mind jeered, while her heart trembled and her body was flooded with the echoes of the sensations he had made her feel.

It was almost as though, like the heroine of a fairy-tale, she was the victim of a powerful spell.

Nonsense, her brain denied acidly. Just because she had reacted sexually to the man, that was no reason to go investing him with magical powers.

Sex. A sad smile curled her mouth. Paul had accused her of being almost completely lacking in sexuality. She was cold and frigid, he had complained when she had refused to go away with him. Didn't she realise how much he wanted her? Well, now she knew the true depth of that wanting, and it had been a very shallow need indeed. A need which, she suspected, would have been quickly quenched if she had given way to him.

Hopefully her response to Luke Chalmers was the same; something which would quickly fade if she ignored it and refused to give in to its insidious demand. A fire which would die down as quickly as it had arisen if she smothered it with common sense and hard reality.

And if she didn't? She stood still, gazing blindly towards the empty fireplace, her heart thudding erratically, her whole body suddenly bathed in a fierce heat.

This was all nonsense, she told herself firmly. She would probably not even see the man again.

When he only lived less than half a mile away at the end of the lane?

He was here to work... just as she was herself. There was no real need for their paths to cross again, and, after all, wouldn't it be better if they did not? The last thing she needed right now was the kind of highly charged sexual affair she was pretty sure was all he had to offer her.

The most sensible thing she could do was to forget she had ever met him and concentrate on all the work that lay in front of her, beginning right now by returning to those gardening books.

Louise had expressed doubt when Melanie had told her that she intended to tackle the wilderness that was the garden by herself, demurring that she felt that Melanie ought to ask around to see if there wasn't someone in the village who could give her some help

'The lawn will have to be scythed,' she had warned Melanie, 'and that's no job for an amateur. And if you do intend to try and grow some salad stuff and soft fruits you'll need someone to dig over the vegetable beds for you.'

'I'm not sure if I can afford to employ someone to do that.' Melanie had hesitated, not wanting to explain to Louise her reluctance to touch a penny of the capital she had inherited, wanting to donate it in its entirety to some deserving charity, which was why she had insisted on paying for her small car out of her own savings.

She wasn't too worried about finding a new job once the summer was over. Without being vain, she knew she was a good secretary with excellent qualifications, and if the worst came to the worst she could always do some temping for a few months until the right job turned up.

In the meantime...in the meantime... She took a deep breath. In the meantime she had better get down to reading her way through that very large pile of books.

Melanie didn't go to bed until very late, determined to exorcise the memory of Luke Chalmers by forcing herself to concentrate on her reading. Eventually it had worked, after a fashion, although unfortunately it hadn't been the chapters on vegetable growing which had caught her attention, but those on the flower borders traditional to cottage gardens, and she hadn't been able to stop herself from daydreaming about how her own garden might look, transformed into such a vision of delight, its lawns smooth and green, its borders filled with silky-petalled poppies, the tall spires of dark blue delphiniums, the sturdiness of lupins and monkshood and the delicacy of the old-fashioned single-coloured 'granny's bonnets' growing against a background of climbing roses and everlasting sweet peas. There would be a lavender hedge edging the path down to the front gate, mingling their scent with the rich clove-like perfume of the pinks that grew between them.

Dizzy with the headiness of her thoughts and plans, she went upstairs, and yet ironically, instead of dreaming of the perfection of the garden she wanted to create, she dreamed instead of Luke Chalmers.

She woke up late, heavy-eyed with an aching head and a dull sense of bewilderment and confusion. Her dreams had disturbed her, leaving her feeling edgy and insecure.

Her bout of flu had robbed her of her appetite, making her lose weight so that Louise had clucked her tongue and warned her that she needed to eat more.

Melanie knew it was true, but she had no appetite for the toast she had made for herself, pushing the plate away with the bread barely touched. She was just sipping her coffee when the phone rang.

Her heart jolted to a standstill and then started to race so much that she was actually trembling as she went to answer it.

Why on earth she should think it might be Luke Chalmers she had no idea, but when she recognised that the male voice on the other end of the line belonged to a stranger, it wasn't relief she felt, but something paralysingly close to disappointment.

'Miss Foden?' the caller enquired a second time, causing her to swallow hard and reply in the affirmative. 'You don't know me. My name is Hewitson, David Hewitson. Shortly before his death, John Burrows and I were having discussions about the sale of the cottage and the land to me. John had, in actual fact, accepted my offer, sensibly realising that he had reached an age at which it was no longer wise for him to live in such isolation. In fact, if it hadn't been for his death, the sale would have gone through.'

Listening to him, Melanie frowned. For some reason, despite his calm, almost gentle voice, she felt as though David Hewitson was almost issuing a subtle threat against her; perhaps even suggesting that by rights he ought to be the owner of the cottage. Her frown deepened. The solicitors had said nothing to her about any such sale, which surely they would have done had it been so advanced that the actual paying over of the money was virtually only a final formality.

What they had said was that there had been several offers of purchase, which might or might not have been motivated by the fact that a proposed new motorway, if approved, could add dramatically to the cottage's land value.

'What I should like to do,' David Hewitson was continuing smoothly, 'is to call round to see you. I'm sure a girl such as yourself would much rather have a few hundred thousand in the bank than a decaying old cottage.'

It was said carelessly, arrogantly, contemptuously almost, so that Melanie felt an atavistic reaction to his suggestion so sharp and intense that it was almost as though she already knew and disliked the man. And yet she had never met him; knew nothing whatsoever about him, and for all she knew her benefactor might genuinely have come to some kind of gentleman's agreement with him concerning the sale of the cottage prior to his death. In which case, surely she ought to honour it?

'Yes, with that kind of capital behind you, a girl as clever as you could go a long way.' There was a brief soft laugh. 'After all, a girl clever enough to get an old skinflint like Burrows to leave her every penny he possessed must surely be wasting her talents in an out of the way village like Charnford.'

Melanie froze, unable to believe what she was hearing, what he was implying. Her body went cold and then hot as her skin crawled with revulsion and disgust. Her hand started to shake as she wondered sickly how many other people had jumped to that same horrible conclusion.

Summoning up every ounce of self-control she could, she said shakily, 'I don't think there's any point whatsoever in your calling, Mr Hewitson. You see, I have no intention of selling either the cottage or the land.'

'But Burrows and I had an agreement——'

'Which, being merely verbal, is not legally binding,' Melanie told him with what she hoped was conviction. Not for the world was she going to lower herself to deny the horrible untrue allegations he had made about her relationship with John Burrows, who had been only a few days short of his eightieth birthday when he died. Instead she said quietly, 'Goodbye, Mr Hewitson.'

She was just on the point of replacing the receiver when the mask of cordiality was stripped from his voice to reveal its true acid venom as he told her savagely, 'You think you're being very clever, don't you, trying to push up the price? Well, let me tell you, you're playing a very dangerous game, little lady. A very dangerous game.'

She slammed down the receiver again without speaking to him again. She was shaking all over, as much with revulsion as anything else. His threat had barely sunk into her awareness. She was far too sickened by his earlier imputation about the reason why she had inherited John Burrows's estate to be aware of anything else.

It was well over an hour before she felt calm enough to pick up the receiver and dial the number of the solicitors.

When she got through to the partner who had dealt with John Burrows's affairs, she asked him without ceremony, almost brusquely, if he knew anything about an agreement John Burrows might have made to sell the cottage to David Hewitson.

When the solicitor confirmed that he had no knowledge of any such agreement, she discovered that she had actually been holding her breath. Had his reply been the opposite, she would have felt that she had no alternative but to allow the sale to go through, since it would have been what her benefactor had intended.

'Why do you ask?' the solicitor enquired.

Briefly she told him, leaving out David Hewitson's imputations about her relationship with John Burrows.

'Mm. David Hewitson is a very well-known local builder with a somewhat unsavoury reputation for the methods his company sometimes uses to acquire building land. It hasn't been unknown for the company to buy property with a preservation order on it and for that property to be accidentally destroyed, thus freeing the land for redevelopment.

'From what I know of Mr Burrows, he would not have taken kindly to a man of David Hewitson's stamp, but of course if you decide to sell out to him . . .'

'No; no, I won't,' Melanie assured him, adding fiercely, 'I'd rather keep the cottage myself than do that.'

'Well, I certainly wouldn't advise you to rush into any hasty decision to sell,' the solicitor warned her. 'Should this proposed new motorway be approved, the value of your land will rise dramatically which is, no doubt, why David Hewitson is so eager to acquire it now.'

After she had replaced the receiver, Melanie stared out into the garden, shivering as she realised that where she had envisaged her green lawns and colourful borders David Hewitson probably planned destruction.

She had become ridiculously attached to the cottage, protective of it almost. It was as though they were kindred spirits in their need for love and care, and as she looked round the dirty cream walls of her sitting-room she had a mental vision of how the room could look, its walls repainted, its beams cleaned and polished, its floor covered, not in the grimy oilcloth that covered it now, but in a rough-textured plain cream carpet, its plainness broken up by the richness of warm oriental rugs, its shabby furniture re-covered, crisp curtains hanging at the windows and perhaps a pretty antique table set in front of the window seat, with a large jug of flowers on it ... flowers from her garden.

A faint sigh escaped her lips. What she was imagining was a daydream, nothing more. She was not here to turn the cottage into her dream home—the kind of home that cried out for a family, *her* family—but simply to make it saleable as a home for someone else.

She had walked across to the window, and now she touched one of the heavy glass panes, rubbing the dirt away from it as she tried to banish the sore place in her heart.

What was she doing, allowing herself to fall into such foolish daydreams? Daydreams which not only included the cottage, but also a man and his children; and not just any man. Her whole body trembled as she tried to deny her mental vision of Luke Chalmers...of the two children which were miniature replicas of the man.

Beyond the leaded windows fitful beams of spring sunshine highlighted the tangled overgrown garden. Louise was right; she could never tackle that wilderness outside on her own. She would *have* to make enquiries in the village to see if she could find someone to help her. And as for the cost...

She had always been thrifty with her money, a habit instilled in her during her days in the children's home. With no one to depend on other than herself, she had soon learned to be sensible with her money.

Her small savings were her only precious security, and yet she felt within her, far more powerful and strong than her desire to protect that security, a deep-seated need to give the cottage every chance she could to prove to the world that it was worthy of being loved...of being cared for...of being preserved.

There was a small dull ache in Melanie's heart. Wasn't she really trying to prove to the world that *she* was worthy of being loved...of being wanted?

She pushed the thought away. It was pointless, giving in to that kind of introspection. She had work to do; but as she walked upstairs she paused, her heart suddenly sinking as she wondered how many other people shared David Hewitson's view of her...how many of the villagers who had outwardly been so pleasant to her were actually inwardly thinking...

Stop that, she warned herself. Stop it at once.

Upstairs in the bedroom, she surveyed the wall and its two strips of wallpaper. Something was definitely wrong—even she could see that—but what? She needed a plumb-line as Luke Chalmers had said. She frowned a little, trying to remember what exactly he *had* said to her. She had done the best she could, scrupulously and meticulously fitting her first piece of paper into the exact angle of the wall, but even she could see that in doing so she had made a mistake.

The wallpaper would have to come off. It was just as well that she had bought a couple of extra rolls to allow for mistakes.

She had just started work when she heard the doorbell. Frowning, she stood still. What if David Hewitson had ignored her rejection and had after all come round in an attempt to persuade her to sell out to him?

Well, if he had, he would very soon learn his mistake, she decided angrily as she marched downstairs.

But when she opened the front door the man standing there was instantly recognisable, her heart rocketing about inside her chest as he smiled down at her and said softly, 'Hello, again. Can I come in?'

Luke. Luke was here. Her heart was ricocheting around inside her chest like a rubber ball; she felt sick and giddy, light-headed and ridiculously, impossibly happy.

'Er—yes... Is it the phone again?' she asked him breathlessly as she turned back into the hallway and he followed her.

'Actually, no. I'm at a bit of a loose end this morning, and I thought I'd come over and give you a hand with that decorating.'

Melanie gaped at him. 'But that's——'

'Very neighbourly of me,' he supplied for her.

She had been about to say that it was totally unnecessary, but now she stared uncertainly at him and said hesitantly, 'It's very kind of you, but there's really no need——'

'Oh, yes, there is,' he contradicted her, adding teasingly, 'I can see you aren't used to decorating. The way you were doing it, anyone sleeping in that room would wake up seasick. Always lived at home up until now, have you?' he suggested casually, heading for the stairs. 'I'm surprised your family has let you come and live in such an isolated spot all on your own.'

Her heart was thumping frantically. As always she felt a mixture of panic and shame fill her at the thought of having to admit that she had no family. A feeling of guilt, as though she were somehow to blame... as though her lack of family somehow made her a second-class citizen.

The years of institutionalised living had left their mark, and a very deep sense of loss and pain that no amount of mature logic could entirely overcome.

'There really is no need for you to do this,' she repeated huskily, ignoring his question about her family.

If he was aware that her avoidance was deliberate he gave no sign of it, telling her cheerfully, 'None at all, other than the fact that it gives me the opportunity to be with you.'

Before she could react to such a blatant piece of flattery he added thoughtfully, 'In fact, I'd have thought you'd have preferred to hire a decorator.'

'I wanted to do it myself,' Melanie told him, unwilling to admit that it was necessity as much as anything else that forced her to tackle the redecoration herself.

'Really? Personally I've always found that when it comes to wallpapering two pairs of hands are always better than one.'

He had reached the top of her stairs and, even though he had only been in the house once before and then only briefly, he seemed to know instinctively which door to open.

But, then, in his job Melanie imagined that he must need to have a good eye for details and the memory to go with it. She wondered what had made him choose such a career. A private detective. She had always imagined such men as small, anonymous characters who could slip unnoticed about their business. He was anything but unnoticeable.

'Mm,' was all he said as he surveyed her attempts to remove the crooked pieces of wallpaper. 'If I could make a suggestion?'

Melanie waited, realising that he was going to do so whether or not she gave him her permission.

'Because of the slope of the ceiling and the dormer windows, it might be an idea to take the paper right up over the wall, along the ceiling and down the other side. A room like this would probably at one time have had a dado rail at chair

height. We could, if you like, break up the busy-
ness of the floral paper by fixing a new rail and
taking the patterned paper down to that level, and
then putting a toning plain paper on the lower half
of the walls.'

We ... Was there any sweeter or more emotive
word in the English language, especially when it
encapsulated the two of them in a small private
circle of intimacy, when it seemed to bond him to
her almost, when it seemed to suggest that
he——?

With a tiny gasp of shock, Melanie shook herself
free of the insidious pull of her own weakness, and
said breathlessly, 'I don't think I could tackle that
kind of thing ... and ...'

'No need. I wasn't suggesting you should,' he
told her drily. When she made no response, he told
her casually, 'Look, this case I'm working on down
here has gone off the boil a bit, so to speak, and
I'm likely to have some time on my hands. How
would it be if I took over as your decorator?'

'Oh, but I couldn't let you do that,' Melanie ob-
jected, but her heart was racing with frantic excitement as she acknowledged how much she
already wanted the dangerous intimacy he was
promising her.

'At least not without ... not without paying you.'

'Paying me?' Suddenly he was frowning at her,
his eyes curiously cold where they had been warm.
The way he was looking at her made her shiver as
she reacted automatically to the sharpness of his
voice by stepping back from him.

It seemed he had read the meaning of her body
language because immediately his expression
changed, his eyes softening back to their original

warmth. 'I'm sorry. It's just that . . . well, the kind
of relationship I had in mind for us wasn't exactly
one of business. However, if you really feel you
have to offer me some form of repayment, how
about payment in kind?'

She couldn't help it. She looked immediately and
betrayingly at his mouth, blushing vividly as she
remembered how it had felt against her own. It was
a very masculine mouth. Looking at it made her
tremble inside and dig her teeth quite sharply into
her own bottom lip, as she fought to banish the
dangerous images tormenting her senses.

'If you would agree to allow me to use your
phone until my own is installed, that would be more
than payment enough,' she heard Luke saying, and
instantly her fair skin flamed with guilty heat as
she prayed that he hadn't realised what she had been
thinking.

Desperate to distract his attention, as if she were
a vulnerable creature of the wild seeking sanctuary,
she said quickly, 'That's . . . that's fine by me. But
this dado rail; do you really think——?'

'I'm sure of it,' he interrupted her. 'Come over
here and look at these marks on the wall.'

In order to do as he suggested she would have to
stand so close to him that their bodies would be
touching. A small shudder of sensation burned
through her and she knew that if she did as he
suggested, if she felt the heat and strength of his
flesh against her own, she would be helpless to
control the foolish response of her own flesh.

'Yes, I can see them from here,' she fibbed,
adding nervously, 'What do you suppose happened
to it—the rails?'

'Who knows? The old boy who used to live here probably ripped them out and used them as firewood,' he told her wryly.

Melanie frowned. How had he known about John Burrows? Almost instantly she chided herself. Why shouldn't he know? But did that mean that he knew about her, about how she had inherited the cottage? But no, he couldn't do so, otherwise he would not have asked her about her family.

'Right, then, let's get started, shall we?'

At one o'clock, with three strips of immaculately aligned paper adorning the ceiling, Melanie suggested hesitantly, 'Would you care for some lunch? It's only salad and cold meat.'

'Sounds like a great idea, but I've got a better one. Why don't you let me drive you into Chester? There's a good DIY place there where we can get the rail, and we could stop somewhere on the way for something to eat to save you doing anything.'

Melanie opened her mouth to ask him how he knew about the DIY centre and then closed it again, telling herself that she of all people ought to know better than to pry into someone else's life, and, taking her silence as acceptance of his suggestion, Luke said warmly, 'Good, that's all settled, then. If I could just use your bathroom to clean up a bit?'

'Er—yes, of course.'

The bathroom was shabby and uncomfortable like the rest of the house. It was also cluttered with her personal toiletries, her make-up and her hairbrush, since it was the only room in the house with a decent mirror in it.

Perhaps she was being foolish and naïve to be embarrassed as she thought of him seeing such intimate possessions, and she had no doubt at all that he would be openly amused if he could read her mind; but the idea of any man—but especially this man—using the room which she considered to be her most personal domain brought a tingle of dangerous sensation racing down her spine.

As he washed his hands free of the sticky wallpaper paste, would he visualise her in the small confines of the bathroom, stepping out of the large old-fashioned bath, her body slick and wet?

The shock of her own thoughts was mirrored in her eyes as she turned quickly away from him.

What on earth was happening to her? She had never had these kinds of thoughts before. Never. They both shocked and excited her, opening secret doors within herself which she had never even known existed.

'The bathroom,' Luke reminded her quietly.

'Oh, yes.' She told him where it was, and then hurried into her own bedroom. It had a narrow single bed, a small chest of drawers and a wardrobe that wobbled because it was missing one foot. It also had a tarnished mirror into which she peered rather desperately after she had changed her jeans and top for a more formal pleated skirt and a toning jumper.

She didn't have a lot of clothes, and most of those she did own had been chosen with her job in mind rather than for attracting admiring males' glances.

Luckily she had washed her hair that morning and it hung in a clean, sweet-swelling, shiny fall on to her shoulders. She frowned as she stared at herself, wishing despairingly that she was taller and prettier, that her hair was curly and her nose straight.

Then she heard the bathroom door open and she grabbed the jacket she had put on the bed and hurried out to meet Luke on the landing.

Was it her imagination, or did his glance linger for just a split second longer than necessary on the soft swell of her breasts? Was that why they seemed so oddly tender as though they had actually been caressed and aroused by the firmness of a man's hands?

'If you're ready,' Luke was saying politely beside her as she battled against the shocking wantonness of her thoughts.

'Er—yes . . . yes . . . I am.'

CHAPTER THREE

'TELL me something about yourself.'

She was sitting in the passenger seat of Luke's car while he drove them towards Chester. His question unnerved her, tightening her defences. She remembered how, over the years, she had been subject to a great many unkind comments because of her orphaned state, especially when she was at school. They had hurt, those comments, leaving tender scars.

'There isn't very much to tell.' She hesitated, her mouth dry as she fought with her reluctance to reveal her own vulnerabilities to him.

There was a small silence during which he gave her a discomfitingly sharp look before saying, 'Or not much you want to tell.'

He was shrewd, she had to give him that, but then his job would of course incline him to look beneath the surface, to probe and go on probing, to query and question.

She was starting to feel uncomfortably conscious of how little she would want to be the subject of his enquiries. Not that she had ever done anything in her life that would make her of any interest to a private detective.

'I hope that one of those things you don't want to tell me isn't that you've got a husband and half a dozen offspring hidden away somewhere.'

His voice sounded lighter, teasing, but even so the shock of his charge caused her to turn automatically towards him, denying, 'No, of course it isn't.'

'So you're not married then, or otherwise involved?'

The look he gave her made her heart turn over. Even though she warned herself that she was being a fool, exposing herself to heaven alone knew what potential danger and unhappiness, she heard herself saying huskily, 'No. No, I'm not.'

'That's something else we share in common, then,' he told her, but before she could question him, could ask exactly what else it was they shared, he was adding more briskly, 'This looks like the turn-off coming up for the DIY place.'

It was, and the next ten minutes were mundanely occupied with following the steady stream of traffic, all of which apparently was heading for the same destination, and then turning into the huge flat wasteland of tarmac dotted with the multi-coloured metal shapes of the many already parked cars.

How unpleasant it looked; how harsh on eyes which had all too quickly become accustomed to the softer, gentle shades in which nature clothed her landscape.

Melanie had always thought of herself as a city person, or at least a suburbanite, and yet already, as Luke parked the car and she got out, she felt exposed, vulnerable, missing the security of her new background into which she seemed to blend so comfortably and easily.

'Not exactly a thing of beauty, is it?' Luke commented wryly, quite obviously reading her thoughts. 'Never mind; it shouldn't take us long to get what we need, and then on to Chester. Have you visited the city at all?'

'No,' Melanie told him. He was walking very close to her, far closer than she would have normally liked, and yet she found that she was actually enjoying the sensation of having him at her side, that she actually almost wanted to close the very small distance which existed between them and walk even nearer to him.

Almost as though in denial of what she was feeling, her brain urged her to move away from him, to remember Paul and the pain he had caused her.

She was not good at judging men and their sincerity or otherwise. Luke's whole manner towards her from the moment they had met suggested that he was an accomplished flirt. And yet . . . and yet there had been that moment in the car when he had looked at her, so seriously, so steadily, so much as though he wanted to convey to her that, given time, there could be far more than a flirtation between them, that her heart had turned over.

'Something wrong?'

She stopped in mid-step and focused on Luke's face. Her heart jumped into a panicky defensive rhythm. How long had he been watching her? What had he seen in her unguarded expression? She must not forget that he was an expert in reading people's expressions; that it was his job to question what lay beneath the surface.

'No,' she assured him quickly, her gaze dropping from his as she started walking again.

'So you weren't perhaps wondering if *I* had a wife and half a dozen children tucked away somewhere, then?' he quizzed her.

This time she managed to not stop walking, but her face burned with heat and she longed for the *savoir-faire* to shrug her shoulders and demand lightly, 'Why should I care?' even while she knew that she *did* care and that in that caring lay a far greater danger than any she had experienced in her relationship with Paul.

The panic inside her grew. This was too much; too soon; she didn't want to feel like this, didn't want the placid calm of her life disrupted by this man and the emotions he aroused within her. Part of her wanted to run and hide from him, to shut him out of her life and to keep him shut out before it was too late. But too late for what?

'As I've already said,' Luke was telling her gently, 'I'm not committed to anyone else, either legally or morally.'

'Just to your work and your client,' Melanie suggested, trying to inject a lighter note into the conversation, and yet it seemed she had said the wrong thing because Luke stopped walking, and when she turned to look at him there was such a different expression on his face, such a stern darkness in his eyes that it was almost like looking at a different man; a far more austere and intimidating man than the one she had previously been allowed to see... Her stomach muscles tensed: *allowed* to see.

Why did she have this odd perception that there was far more to Luke than he was letting her see, and why should it unnerve her so much? As though he sensed her disquiet and wanted to dismiss it, he told her easily, 'My work *is* important to me; after all, it is what pays the bills and keeps a roof over my head.'

'Have you always been a private detective?'

Something warned her that he didn't want her asking him that kind of question, but to do so was safer, surely, than allowing him to probe into *her* history, even if in doing so she was creating a barrier between them.

Normally so sensitive about her own dislike of talking about her past that she never brazenly asked questions of others, now she discovered that she was holding her breath, wondering what Luke would tell her, whether indeed he would tell her anything at all, or simply change the subject.

There was a rather long pause, and she had just decided that he was going to refuse to answer her question when he said slowly, 'No, not always. I was in the army for a time—a family tradition.'

'You didn't like it?' she invited softly when she saw the shadows darkening his eyes.

'What I didn't like was seeing people—friends—die,' he told her curtly. 'I stuck it out long enough to appease my pride and the family honour, and then when I came out I joined forces with a friend and we set up in business together.'

So he wasn't merely working for a detective agency; he was one of the partners in it.

'Any more questions?'

She started to shake her head and then said quickly, 'Have you . . . have you any family?'

'Sort of. I was an only child. My father was in the army. He was killed in action when I was very young——'

'Your—your mother?' Melanie queried eagerly, interrupting him. What if, after all, she could confide in him? What if, like her, he knew what it meant not to have a home to call his own? Not to have a past . . . a history? But then she realised that, even if his mother was no longer alive, his past was not really like hers. The way he had talked of joining the army hinted at family traditions, an awareness of belonging, of being part of an established family unit, whereas she...

She knew nothing other than that her young parents had been killed together in a car crash; that she had been saved and that the authorities had not been able to trace any kind of family connections on either her mother's or her father's side.

'My mother is very much alive. She remarried a few years ago.'

Again his eyes darkened, and Melanie wondered sympathetically if he had resented that remarriage, although she guessed that he was somewhere in his early thirties, and that surely meant that he must have been old enough at the time of her remarriage to accept taking second place in her life.

'She lives in Canada now. Neil, her husband, was a widower with three daughters and a son, and, as my mother keeps pointing out to me, I'm the eldest and as yet I'm the only one who has failed to present them with a grandchild.'

'What excuse do you give her?' Melanie asked him teasingly.

They had just reached the large purpose-built superstore. People were coming and going busily through the glass doors, and yet she was totally oblivious to them; to everything other than the man standing so close to her, as Luke responded devastatingly, 'I used to tell her, quite truthfully, that I'm waiting for the right woman to come along.'

Her heart was pounding frantically. He couldn't really mean what he appeared to be saying to her. She must be imagining things. He couldn't really be looking at her like that...as though...

Almost running in her haste to escape from her own dangerous thoughts, she bolted for one of the doors, but somehow Luke got there before her, holding it open for her, taking hold of her arm as he guided her through it, making her feel somehow precious and cherished . . . making her feel . . . To her dismay she could feel the prickle of emotional tears stinging her eyes.

After Paul's cruelty, Luke's tenderness made her feel frighteningly vulnerable. Paul had opened her eyes to the fact that men could lie so convincingly that you didn't know they had lied until it was almost too late.

But why should Luke lie to her? Why should he pretend to want her company? To pretend to want her? He could of course simply be aiming to idle away time he would otherwise have spent simply waiting for his telephone to be installed, but he must surely have realised by now that she was no sophisticate; that she was not a suitable candidate to play opposite him in a practised game of flirtation and seduction.

The trouble was that he was a man totally outside her limited experience. No, she corrected herself; the trouble was that she was already dangerously vulnerable to him and had been from the moment he had kissed her.

She tensed as she felt his hand on her arm, wondering if he had somehow read her mind, if he was actually going to kiss her again right here in this crowded building; but as she turned towards him she realised that he was simply trying to bring her attention to the directions hanging above their heads.

'I suspect we need to go this way,' he informed her.

The DIY centre was a whole new world to Melanie. She stared around, bemused and confused, while Luke assembled everything he thought they would need.

Only when they had come to the check-out and he reached for his cheque-book did Melanie gather her wits sufficiently to refuse to allow him to pay. She half expected him to get annoyed, but to her relief he immediately accepted her protest and allowed her to pay for the things herself.

He was, she saw as she wrote out the cheque, almost as surprised by her determination to pay as she had been by his acceptance of it.

Was he only used, then, to women who expected a man always to do the paying? Her own life had been far too hard for her to know anything other than the necessity of supporting herself, and, while she sometimes wondered wistfully what it would be like to have some indulgent male picking up the bills for her, in her heart of hearts she acknowledged that she prized her independence far too much to ever really enjoy that kind of role. She believed in men and women being equal, being partners, each one supporting the other—or, rather, each one *prepared* to support the other if necessary, but also prepared to allow the other their individual independence. That was the only way to maintain respect within a relationship, to keep it wholesome and healthy.

However, having won her battle to pay for her goods, she made no demur when Luke offered to carry them to the car for her.

'Lunch now,' he suggested, once her purchases were safely stowed away, 'and then back to your place to start work.'

'This really is very kind of you,' Melanie told him uncertainly. 'It really isn't...you don't have to...'

'I don't have to what?' he asked her as they got into the car. 'I don't have to spend my time with an extremely beautiful woman?'

Melanie flushed brilliantly, opening her mouth to protest that she wasn't beautiful, and then closed it again.

'That's better,' he approved as he set the car in motion. 'I can see that your mother must have told you never to argue with a man when he's driving.'

'I don't have a mother.'

The bleak statement was made before she could check it and, as the hot, shocked colour stormed her skin and then receded from it, she wondered what on earth had possessed her to make such an admission.

It was too late to call it back now. Even without turning her head to look at him, she knew that Luke was watching her. Another moment and he would be questioning her; then would come the shock, the surprise, the distaste.

Before she could stop herself, she said fiercely, 'I don't have a father, either; in fact I don't have *anyone*—no parents, no siblings, no one.'

There, it was out...said, the dreaded fact falling into its usual abyss of shocked silence. She had learned a long time ago that to admit her orphaned state was tantamount to admitting to having a criminal record or an unspeakable social disease; as shocking to her onlookers as though she had stripped herself naked in front of them and then revelled in their embarrassment. And people *were* embarrassed by her revelations; she knew that; knew it from the way they looked at her; the way they backed off and then turned away from her.

There was no reason why Luke should be any different.

She heard him repeating her words, heard the shock in them; felt her heart sink, and the nausea begin to churn inside her; but then, shockingly, unexpectedly, the car stopped and his hand cupped her jaw, his fingers sliding into her hair as he turned her head round so that he could look at her.

This wasn't what normally happened... This was confusing her... bemusing her, or was it the sensual heat of Luke's hand against her skin, his fingers gently massaging the tense skin of her scalp? ... a reflex and automatic action she was most sure he had no idea he was performing, because when her startled gaze met his he was watching her with a sombreness that was totally non-sexual.

'No one,' he repeated, frowning a little. 'I hadn't realised. I suppose that explains——'

He stopped abruptly, but Melanie could guess what he had been about to say.

'Why I didn't want to talk about my background when you asked me earlier. It's very difficult to talk about something of which you have no knowledge whatsoever.'

She was starting to tremble; she could feel the old anguish, the old sickness rising up inside her. Another few seconds and she would be completely unable to control what she was feeling.

She forced herself to remember how tremulously she had confided to Paul about her past, how she

had waited for his sympathy, his concern, how she
had held her breath, aching for him to take her in
his arms, to kiss her and tell her that it didn't
matter, that she had him to love her now; but instead he had turned away from her; instead he had
been as shocked and filled with distaste as all the
others.

'Can we please go now?'

Her teeth were chattering and she was starting to
shake. She felt Luke's hand tighten against her skin
as though he meant to refuse to let her go, and then
almost immediately its grip was relaxed.

'Yes,' he agreed quietly. 'This isn't a subject to
be discussed here. I'm sorry if I upset you. I do
know what it's like. At least, a little. For years I
believed that in some way I was responsible for my
father's death; that it was because I was unsatis-
factory as a son in some way that he had been killed.
My mother was horrified when she eventually realised what I thought. I understand that children
with parents who are divorcing suffer the same
feeling, that somehow they are to blame for the
break-up of their parents' marriages.'

He was setting the car in motion again and as he
did so he asked her quietly, 'You say you have no
other family. Are you sure—have you ...?'

'The authorities made all the usual enquiries.
They couldn't trace anyone. It isn't as unusual a
situation as you might think; children's homes all
over the country——' She stopped abruptly,
knowing that she was allowing her emotions to get
out of hand. 'I'm sorry,' she apologised to him.

When he suggested briefly, 'Would you prefer to
give Chester a miss and go straight home?' it was
only her pride—plus the fact that she was practi-

cally biting through her bottom lip—that prevented her from allowing her tears to fall.

She said shakily, 'Yes. I think that would be the best thing.'

So, despite his apparent sympathy, he was just like the others after all. What she had mistaken for concern, for sympathy, had probably only been professional curiosity, hence his question about whether or not she had tried to trace her family. Perhaps he had been hoping to pick up a new commission for his business, she reflected bitterly; he had probably realised by now that that would be a more profitable way of spending the next few days. Yes; she doubted that he would be as keen to pursue his flirtation with her now that he knew the truth.

People like her, people who had been deprived of love during their childhood, had such a dangerous need to be loved that the opposite sex tended to give them a wide berth, especially when a flirtation was all they had in mind. No; she suspected that the few days he had talked of would rapidly coalesce into this afternoon's trip to the superstore and the consequent drive back to her cottage; that Luke would at some point on the return journey discover some vital and hitherto overlooked piece of business which would prevent him from spending the rest of the day with her. And after that... after that she would simply not see him again.

She told herself that it was all for the best; that she was far too vulnerable to share with him the kind of brief meaningless relationship she had no doubt he had originally had in mind; that to be rejected now, while humiliating, was in the long run safer.

It should have come as no real surprise therefore, when, after pulling up outside her cottage after an almost silent drive, Luke should say briefly, 'Look, there's something I've got to do. I'll see you safely inside and then...'

No, it shouldn't have been a surprise. It shouldn't have hurt either, but it did.

All she wanted to do was to escape from him; to escape from everyone; to be on her own, some-where safe, somewhere private; somewhere she could give vent to her pain, her anguish, without anyone else witnessing her lack of self-control.

'There's no need to come to the door with me,' she told Luke tightly, keeping her face averted and her body tensely several feet away from his; but he still kept pace with her, still waiting with apparent courtesy and care while she fumbled for her keys and eventually managed to let herself inside the cottage.

She told herself that she was not going to watch while he drove away. After all, why should she? He was a stranger, anyway; a man she had known for less than twenty-four hours. Known? She smiled bitterly to herself. Was she really never going to learn the true lessons of the past?

Luke had been gone ten minutes before Melanie realised that he still had their afternoon's pur-chases with him. Well, what did it matter? Without his help there was no way she could have fixed the dado rail in place anyway.

In the kitchen she stared dispiritedly at the wall, which slowly started to blur as tears filmed her eyes.

She bit down hard on her bottom lip, tightening her throat muscles against her urge to cry.

Crying didn't help. She had learned that years ago, surely, the first time she realised that she wasn't like other children; that she was different; that she was something called an orphan.

But then she had been a child and she wasn't a child any longer. Now she was an adult; now she had taken control of her life, and it was up to her what she made of it.

All right, so she *had* found Luke Chalmers attractive; when he'd kissed her he had made her feel... She swallowed tautly. Best not to think about how Luke had made her feel when he'd kissed her; best to think instead about how he had made her feel less than half an hour ago, when he had walked her to the cottage door and then left her there, when he had changed his mind about wanting to spend time with her, when he had——

She stiffened suddenly as she heard the sound of a car drawing up outside, watching the window warily. When she saw Luke coming down the path towards the back door, her heart started to thump erratically.

She went to the door and opened it.

'The wood——' she began unceremoniously, but he stopped her, saying cheerfully,

'Oh, that can stay where it is for now. I suddenly remembered when we were on the way back here that there's a shop in the next village where they sell the most marvellous home-made bread and stuff, and I thought that, even though you hadn't felt up to having lunch out, you might fancy afternoon tea. My domestic skills aren't up to much but I am capable of brewing a respectable pot of tea and toasting a few crumpets. That's what I've got here,' he added, brandishing the paper carrier-bag he was holding. 'That, plus some homemade scones and the requisite jam and butter and cream. I even got the tea—Queen Mary's sort, one of my favourites; I hope you'll like it . . .'

Melanie stared at him while her thoughts rushed dizzily through her head.

This couldn't really be happening. She was imagining it . . . hallucinating . . . In real life one simply did not come knocking on her door, offering to make her afternoon tea. Things like this simply did not happen to her.

She closed her eyes and then opened them again very slowly.

Luke was still there, only now, instead of smiling at her, he was watching her with frowning anxiety. 'Is something wrong?'

Wrong . . . wrong . . .

Her mouth had gone dry. She moistened her lips with the tip of her tongue. 'No . . . no,' she said huskily. 'Nothing. Everything's fine.'

And suddenly, gloriously, wonderfully, it was.

She had been wrong about him, wrong about him being just like all the others. Wrong about him rejecting her because of her background . . . wrong about him in every way—except one.

Her body shook as she saw the way he was looking at her, her eyes illuminating brilliantly.

Would he kiss her again . . . ? Would he . . . ?

She came out of her daydreams to hear him saying wistfully, 'I don't suppose that chimney on your roof means that this place still has a genuine, honest-to-goodness, proper fire, does it? There's something about tea, crumpets and a good log fire . . .'

'There *is* a fire,' Melanie agreed shakily. 'But as yet I haven't tried to light it, although I know there are some logs in the garage.'

'Great; leave everything to me.'

CHAPTER FOUR

LEAVE everything to him, Luke had said, and
perhaps weakly—yes, certainly weakly for a very
modern and independent-minded young woman—
Melanie had done exactly that; and now here she
was, sitting opposite him with the fire burning
warmly between them, and the logs—apple logs, he
had told her approvingly—crackling com-
panionably.

It was still light outside but the sky was overcast,
and without the lights on the fire gave the room a
warm glow that softened the shabbiness of its décor
and furnishings.

On the folding table that Melanie had found
tucked away in the walk-in pantry was a tray of tea,
made by Luke, and on the hearth a covered dish
holding the toasted crumpets.

Her appetite, which had fled during those moments in the car when she had revealed to him her
history, had suddenly returned, her mouth water-
ing as Luke offered her the covered plate.

Oozing butter and jam, it was hardly the most
healthy of foods, but it certainly tasted delicious,
she admitted as she sank her teeth greedily into the
crumpet and then closed her eyes as she savoured
its taste.

When she opened them again, Luke was watching
her. The amusement in his eyes made her flush like
a schoolgirl.

'I was hungry,' she told him defensively.

He laughed at her, the sound of his laughter not mocking, but warm and tender. 'Don't apologise. It's a pleasure to see a woman enjoying her food, especially these days. What do you think of the tea?'

She took a sip.

'It's good,' she told him.

He laughed again. 'Don't sound so surprised. My mother is a lifelong tea-drinker. This is one of her favourites.'

An hour and two more crumpets later, Melanie felt as though she couldn't possibly eat another thing.

'Mmm. Me neither,' Luke agreed.

She saw him glance at his watch and felt herself tense as she waited for him to say that he had to leave, but instead he told her, 'We can still manage to put in a couple of hours' work on the decorating if you feel up to it.'

'Well, I can hardly let you start doing that now,' she began to protest, but immediately he overruled her.

'I'm looking forward to it.'

He was smiling at her so warmly that her body seemed to respond of its own accord to that warmth, a gentle tingling beginning at the base of her spine and spreading out to every part of her body.

She got up quickly. This was silly. She was over-reacting, surely. All right, so he was an attractive man; a very attractive man; and so he seemed intent on making her aware that he found her attractive as a woman, but that didn't mean . . .

She reached down to pick up the tray, and then tensed as Luke reached out and caught hold of her right hand. While she looked at him in confusion, he raised it to his mouth, and then, as her stomach muscles clenched and her whole body shuddered inwardly in shocked disbelief, he slowly started to lick her fingers, telling her softly, 'Blackcurrant jam always was my favourite.' And, while his tongue tip probed between her fingers, she looked down at her hand and realised, with a mind that suddenly seemed incapable of assimilating even the most basic of information, that there was indeed jam on her skin. But then, as Luke continued his cleansing operation, her ability to think disintegrated completely beneath the flood of sensation engulfing her like a landslide.

Common sense, caution and the instinct for self-preservation which her life had instilled in her—all of them warned her that she must stop what was happening to her before it was too late, but their urgent voices, even when they called out to her in unison, were not loud enough to drown out the siren song of her own desire.

Desire like this—so fierce, so strong, so urgent and inescapable that she could do nothing other than succumb to its fiery licking heat—was something she had never experienced before, something so new to her in fact that she wasn't even aware of gazing at Luke with dazed, confused eyes, or of reaching out to him with her free hand, an instinctive imploring gesture, pleading cessation of the torment he was causing inside her.

Shudder after shudder trembled through her body; she was breathing unevenly, taking short gulps of air.

'Melanie.'

She heard the raw, fierce note in Luke's voice and focused muzzily on him. He looked different, somehow; the bones in his face seemed harder, sharper, the flesh along his cheekbones burning with heat. He was even looking at her differently. His eyes: she had never seen that look in a man's eyes before; never realised that male desire could actually make the coolest of eyes burn so hot that she could almost see the hungry flames of desire that darkened them.

Even if she had been able to comprehend that he was going to kiss her, she doubted that she would have stopped him; but as it was it seemed to her confused brain that one moment he was releasing her hand and the next she was somehow or other not just in his arms, but locked so tightly against his body that she could almost feel the fierce pulse of his blood through his veins.

This time there was no teasing preparation, no slow, almost careful seduction of her lips. This time his kiss had a hunger, an urgency that made her heart shake and her body yearn.

When he opened her mouth, parting her lips with the powerful thrust of his tongue, the involuntary convulsion of her body elicited a harsh sound of triumph from him that sent warning thrills skittering down her spine.

He made no attempt to touch her intimately, and yet somehow the very way he was kissing her was more of an intimacy than if he had physically caressed her body. Her breasts ached and so did her stomach. With each passionate thrust of his tongue within her mouth she felt a corresponding urge to press herself ever closer to his body, to mould herself to his flesh, his bones, until she was physically a part of him.

One of his hands supported the back of her head, his fingers splayed out against her skull, the other lay against the small of her back, pressing her into his body. Her arms were wrapped around his neck, her fingers curling into solid muscle and taut flesh.

Somewhere in the distance she could hear something, an annoying, intrusive sound, but it was only when Luke released her that she realised that it was her telephone ringing.

When she went to answer it she discovered that she could barely walk, that her whole body felt weak and empty. As she stepped out into the hallway the cool air there made her shiver slightly. She picked up the receiver and said her name. Her voice was croaky, unfamiliar.

'Ah, good. It's David Hewitson here. You may remember. We spoke this morning.'

David Hewitson. It was several seconds before she could pull herself together enough to place the name, and when she did she felt a tight knot of mingled anger and apprehension begin to form in the pit of her stomach.

'I'm sorry, Mr Hewitson,' she began purposefully, 'but I don't really see the point in your call. I'm not prepared to sell the cottage to you. I've been in touch with my solicitor and he has confirmed that he has no record of any agreement made by Mr Burrows to sell the cottage or the land to you.'

There was a brief pause, and then David Hewitson said angrily, 'I've already told you. It was a verbal agreement——'

'I'm sorry, Mr Hewitson,' Melanie cut in. She still couldn't forget the horrid accusations he had made the last time he had telephoned her. Accusations which, like a wasp's sting, had left their poison behind to fester and infect. She knew of course that there was no truth in his allegations, but how many other people shared that knowledge? How many others would prefer to think as David Hewitson plainly did?

'I'm warning you,' he told her, overriding her. 'I want that land and I mean to have it. I'm a realistic man, Miss Foden. I'm prepared to pay a fair price for what I want, but, as I've already said, I'm not a sick old man, easily fooled by a greedy bitch with a pretty face.'

Weak with shock, Melanie replaced the receiver before he could say any more. She felt so ill that she had to lean against the wall while she regathered her physical strength. She was still leaning there when Luke walked out of the sitting-room. He must have heard her replace the receiver, she realised as he came towards her, his forehead creased with concern.

'Something's wrong. What is it...? What?'

'It's nothing... nothing at all,' Melanie fibbed, 'I had flu a short time ago, and it's left me feeling stupidly weak, that's all.'

She didn't know why she was lying to him, why she didn't want to tell him the truth. Or did she? Was it because she was afraid that he, like David Hewitson, would judge her unfairly? But why should she have that fear? There was no reason.

'Is that why you bought this place? Somewhere to rest and recuperate?'

'I—I didn't buy the cottage. I—I inherited it.' She forced herself to make the admission.

She couldn't look at him; her stomach was all screwed up in tight apprehensive knots.

'You inherited it? But I thought you said you had no family...'

She bit down hard on her bottom lip. 'Yes. Yes, I did.'

'I see. The previous owner was an old friend, then, someone you were close to?' The voice was suddenly cold, chilling her.

It was a natural enough assumption, and certainly far easier to accept than the truth, which was that she had had absolutely no idea of John Burrows's existence until his solicitors had tracked her down.

She still felt oddly uneasy about her inheritance; still felt as though she was in some way a fraud...as though there had been a mistake and the inheritance had not been meant for her at all. As though somehow she had become tainted by David Hewitson's accusation. *That* was why she couldn't bring herself to tell Luke the truth, and lied huskily instead, 'Yes. Yes, that's right.'

She still couldn't bring herself to look at him. The small hallway seemed to be filled with tension. Probably as a result of her telephone call from David Hewitson, she reflected shakily.

'There's still enough daylight left for me to make a start on the bedroom.' His voice was neutral, soothing her taut nerves.

The bedroom. The swift change of subject bemused her for a moment. She had still barely recovered from the intensity of the passionate kiss they had just shared, and was really in no mood to

consider such mundane things as decorating a
bedroom, but Luke, it seemed, was, and, that being
the case, good manners necessitated that she went
upstairs with him to do what she could to assist.
At least he was no longer questioning her about her
inheritance.

As she watched him work Melanie realised that
he was far more experienced at this sort of thing
than she had at first imagined, his movements deft
and, to her eyes at least, dispiritingly professional
compared with her amateurish attempts to take on
the challenge of the bedroom's sloping, uneven
walls.

He worked hard as well, his manner towards her
almost remote, without any hint of the passion he
had shown her earlier.

She told herself that she was a fool to feel that
there was a change in his manner, a coolness, but
the years and her upbringing had honed her sen-
sitivity to such an extent that she could almost feel
his altered attitude as though it had caused an actual
physical drop in temperature in the air between
them.

What had caused it? Her reaction to his kiss?
Had she been too passionately responsive to him?
She remembered that when he had drawn away
from her, their embrace interrupted by the ring of
the telephone, he had looked at her rather oddly.

At the time she had put that look down to the
fact that he had been as taken off guard by the
passion which had flared between them as she had
been herself. Now she wondered unhappily if she
had perhaps completely misread the situation. After
all, what did *she* know about men or their
emotions?

It was almost dusk before Luke finally announced that it was time to stop work, by which stage most of the walls had been carefully measured and marked where the mouldings would eventually be applied.

'Tomorrow we'll start work on painting the mouldings,' Luke told Melanie. 'With any luck the whole thing should be finished by the end of the week.'

They were halfway downstairs when the telephone started to ring. Melanie felt her body tense with nervous dread. If it was David Hewitson again... But when she reluctantly picked up the receiver she heard a woman's voice on the other end of the line, and the woman asked, or rather demanded, to speak with Luke.

Without asking her name, Melanie handed the receiver to him and then tactfully excused herself, hurrying into the kitchen and closing the door behind her.

The woman, whoever she was, had sounded both aggressive and unpleasant. She had called Luke by his Christian name and had seemed to have no doubts that she would be able to get in touch with him. But that was no reason for Melanie to leap to the conclusion that she was romantically involved with Luke. After all, he had told her himself that he was free of any emotional commitments, giving her that information without her having to seek it.

The phone call didn't last very long. When Luke came into the kitchen, though, he seemed preoccupied and distant. He made no mention of the phone call—and did not proffer an explanation of the identity of the caller—other than to apologise for the fact that he was making use of her telephone.

That was the arrangement they had made, Melanie reminded him stiffly. She was trying to keep her face averted from him. She didn't want him to read in her eyes how upset she was by the way his manner towards her had changed.

As he walked to the door, Luke announced, 'I have to go now, but I'll get here as early as I can in the morning—say, about ten?'

So he still intended to help her with the bedroom. Until that moment she hadn't realised how much she had feared that he might have changed his mind. And that frightened her, knowing how much he had already come to mean to her. Her fear made her protest huskily and protectively, 'It really isn't necessary, you know. You must have far more important things you want to do.'

Her voice didn't sound quite as firm as she would have liked. Indeed, her sensitive ears suspected that there was even a trace of pathos in it.

Luke had been about to open the back door, but now he stopped and turned to look at her. 'More important than spending time with you? Impossible.'

Once again his voice was soft with warmth, his eyes dark with emotion. Once again she was bewildered and caught off guard by the change in him.

'I'm sorry if I upset you earlier today when I asked about your past . . . your family.'

'I—I wasn't upset.'

It was a lie and they both knew it.

Luke took a step towards her and she took one back. She felt the edge of the kitchen table against her spine. If he came any closer to her he would be close enough to kiss her. For some reason that knowledge made her panic.

'I haven't been entirely alone anyway. I've been lucky enough to have good friends.' She was gabbling, making conversation simply to fill the tense silence, and she was hardly telling the truth. The closest friends she had were Louise and her husband, and then only because Louise had persisted and broken her way through Melanie's barriers of shyness and self-defence which put off others; but for some reason her stammered comment made Luke stiffen and stare almost angrily at her.

'Yes, you have, haven't you?' he agreed quietly, but it wasn't a pleasant quietness, and it was only when he had actually gone and the door had closed behind him that Melanie realised that there had almost been something faintly cynical about it.

He confused her totally with abrupt and, to her eyes, illogical changes of mood; one moment he could be tender, caring, making her feel that he felt drawn to her with the same deep compulsion she felt for him, and yet almost in the same breath he could distance himself from her so completely that she felt almost as though he actually disliked her. She couldn't understand it at all.

As she made herself a cup of coffee she acknowledged, as she had done the previous evening, that the safest thing for her might be to call a halt to what was happening between them right now, to tell him when he arrived tomorrow morning that she had changed her mind about allowing him to use her phone, and that she no longer required or wanted his assistance with her decorating.

Yes, that was what she *ought* to do, but would she have the strength to actually do it?

* * *

During the evening the telephone rang. Melanie hesitated for a long time before lifting the receiver, licking her dry lips with a nervous tongue tip, her tension evaporating when she heard Louise's familiar voice.

'You took your time! I was just beginning to think you had gone out. How's the decorating going?'

Uncertainly Melanie explained what had happened to her.

'And this man...this Luke has offered to help out with your decorating in return for being allowed to use your phone? That's great! I wonder what sort of case he's working on...' Louise mused. 'Probably a divorce. Horrid, really. I'd hate the thought of being involved in such unhappiness. But tell me a bit more about him. What's he like? Is he good-looking?'

She laughed when Melanie was very hesitant in her reply.

'Mm...like that, is it?' she teased knowingly. 'Well, I hope you haven't told him about your lovely windfall. Oh, heavens, Mel, I didn't mean that the way it sounds,' she added hurriedly. 'I wasn't meaning to suggest that he might be some kind of fortune-hunter. I suppose that it's just that you're such a trusting innocent that I feel I have to keep reminding you that there are far too many big bad wolves prowling around, looking for tender little morsels like you to gobble up.'

'We haven't really talked about it,' Melanie told her truthfully. 'He knows that I've recently inherited the cottage, but in its present run-down state I suspect he probably thinks it's more of a burden than an asset.'

'Mm. Well, big bad wolves go out on the prowl for more than just money,' Louise warned her, 'and you are a remarkably pretty and desirable young woman.' Melanie felt her heart start to pound, but luckily, before Louise asked her any more questions, she had changed the subject completely, saying, 'Oh, by the way, the reason I'm ringing, apart from checking to make sure you're OK, is to ask if you'd like to have a couple of old wardrobes and a dressing-table we're getting rid of. They belonged to ma-in-law but we've finally decided that we can have new fitted furniture in that room, and I remembered your saying that you were desperately short of furniture for the cottage. Of course, when you sell it you'll probably find the stuff is a bit of a liability, but until then it will at least make the place look a bit more lived in. Anyway, if you want it, Simon says he can bring it over in the van.'

'I'd love it,' Melanie told her gratefully. It was true that the cottage was lamentably short of furniture. The larger of the three bedrooms was very basically furnished with a bed and an old chest of drawers. The second bedroom, which she had adopted as her own, had possessed a very old and unappealing single bed which she had disposed of, buying herself a brand new divan, but making do with the rickety wardrobe and small chest of drawers, and the third room, the one she was presently engaged in decorating, had been filled with an assortment of broken chairs and other pieces of furniture, none of which had appeared to have any charm or value and all of which she had, on Louise's advice, paid a couple of men to come and take away.

She knew the furniture Louise was talking about and, while it was undoubtedly rather old-fashioned and perhaps too heavy for a modern house such as Louise's, she had no doubts whatsoever that it would be completely at home in the cottage.

As she thanked Louise for her generosity she felt a rush of gratitude and affection for her friend, who, she was quite sure, could have sold the bedroom furniture for quite a respectable price had she chosen to do so. However, when she said as much Louise laughed at her. 'Who on earth wants that heavy old stuff these days? It isn't old enough to be antique. It weighs a ton. It needs polishing in the old traditional way, and, besides, I've never been that keen on oak.

'How *is* the decorating going, by the way?' she added, returning to her original question. 'Or are you and this Luke too busy getting to know one another to be making much progress with the wallpapering?'

Not even to Louise did Melanie feel able to admit how very deeply she felt drawn to Luke, especially in view of Louise's earlier warnings; she was able, however, to tell her what Luke had suggested in relation to improving the decorative state of the bedroom, and when she had finished Louise commented approvingly, 'Well, it's a marvellous suggestion, and if he's prepared to help you carry it out... One word of warning though, my love: don't put too much of yourself into all this redecorative work, otherwise when the time comes to sell up you aren't going to want to do so. Mind you, there's nothing to stop you staying on in the cottage. It is a little remote, but with this Luke for a neighbour...'

Melanie could see the way her friend's mind was working and told her quickly, 'Oh, Luke won't be staying long. He's only renting his cottage, and as for me keeping this place...'

She gave a tiny sigh. Even if she should want to stay, even if she had not already decided that the cottage and the land must be sold and the proceeds given to some worthy charity, to go on living here would be impossible. For a start she would need to find herself a job, and that would prove virtually impossible; there was no industry of any sort... no one who might wish to employ a secretary. Unless... There was of course Chester. An hour... just less than an hour's drive away.

'So I'll arrange for Simon to bring this stuff out to you, and then I'll give you a ring to let you know when he's coming,' Louise was saying, and Melanie dismissed her errant thoughts to concentrate on her friend's words.

Later that evening, when the fire had died down and she had eaten her supper, she found herself reliving the events of the day... remembering.

But no, she must not give in to this temptation, this compulsion almost to daydream about Luke, to recall, sensation by sensation, second by second, the time she had spent with him, and how he had made her feel.

She would be far better employed in worrying about David Hewitson's obnoxious call.

She was sure she had not imagined the threat he had made against her. The solicitor had originally suggested when she had told him of her intention to sell the property that she wait until the outcome of the enquiry into the motorway extension was known, and for her to then put both the cottage

and the land up for auction, because that way she
would probably achieve a higher price; and this was
what she had decided to do.

It wasn't that she wanted the money for herself—
far from it—but she suspected intuitively that David
Hewitson had hoped to browbeat her into letting
him have the property and the land at far below its
real market value, and that, thwarted of this goal,
he would probably continue to harass her and to
make his vile insinuations in the hope that she
would eventually give in.

Had she herself been the only person who would
benefit financially from the sale of her inheritance
she might well have done so, but that was not the
case.

Since she had come to live in the cottage she had
realised how very alone and unloved her benefactor
had been, and she had come to feel that her inheritance from him was in some way an almost
sacred trust; that the loneliness, the aloneness they
had both known was an invisible thread that linked
them to one another, just as it linked them to the
many, many other people throughout the country,
throughout the world—people who also knew the
intense emotional deprivation of that deep inner
loneliness which could be worse than the very
hardest kind of financial poverty.

And, that being the case, she owed it both to
John Burrows and to those who would eventually
benefit through her from the sale of his land and
home to get the maximum amount of money she
could from the sale.

Restlessly she wished there was someone she
could confide in; someone she could turn to for
help and support; someone...

No, not just someone, she admitted honestly. The person who came most quickly to mind when she acknowledged this need within herself to reach out for protection and help was Luke Chalmers.

It was ridiculous, allowing herself to harbour these dangerous feelings for him. No matter how much he might intimate that he found her physically desirable, no matter how attractive she herself might find *him*, there was really no excuse for her to feel this aching, yearning need to get closer to him emotionally. Had she really no sense? Had she learned nothing from the past?

CHAPTER FIVE

TODAY, if Luke *did* put in an appearance she would treat him with cheerful friendliness, but if he made any kind of physical overtures to her whatsoever she would very quickly and firmly repel them, Melanie told herself determinedly as she finished her breakfast and cleared away the things.

After all, she had far too much to worry about right now to have the time to spare worrying about her emotional vulnerability to a man she hardly knew.

Just as she had far too much physical work to do to waste one single precious moment of it watching the clock and wondering frantically if Luke was actually going to appear, she admonished herself as she turned her head to glance quickly at the kitchen clock.

But if Luke *didn't* arrive, how would she get the bedroom finished, and...?

If he didn't arrive she had plenty of work to do in the garden, she told herself, and as for the bedroom...well, if the worst came to the worst, she would just have to revert to her original plan of decorating it herself. Granted, she would not be able to make it look as attractive, but at least it would be clean and fresh.

Last night she had told herself that if she never saw Luke again if would probably be for the best, and that opinion still held good.

So why was she tensing her body and glancing so anxiously at the clock? Why was she stretching her ears, trying to catch the sound of an approaching car? Why was she battling against the sharp bitter taste of disappointment and the pain that went with it? Surely not because she wanted to see Luke?

After all, she hardly knew the man. No, her heart corrected her. Her mind hardly knew him, but her body... her senses... She gave a small shudder as she tried to ignore what those same senses were trying to tell her, but they rebelliously refused to be silenced.

He had bewitched them, cast a spell on her stupid vulnerable body and emotions, she told herself angrily. It would serve him right if she took his kisses at face value and allowed herself to believe...

What? That he was falling in love with her? How ridiculous, her brain said scornfully, but where her heart and her emotions were concerned she knew that she was already fighting a rear-guard action, and had been doing so almost from the moment he had first kissed her.

It couldn't be happening like this, she denied frantically. She couldn't be falling in love with him. She wasn't *that* stupid... She had already been hurt once, but instinct warned that the pain she had suffered over Paul would be like a small scratch compared to the mortal wound of the pain which Luke could inflict on her.

At ten-past ten Luke had not arrived. At half-past she suspected that he was not going to do so, but no matter how much she told herself stalwartly that it was all for the best her heart still ached, and when she put on her wellington boots and an old jacket so that she could go out and do some gardening her throat was tight with tears of disappointment and misery.

Once out in the garden it was impossible to know where to begin. What was presumably lawn looked like a field; where there had originally been flowerbeds was now a tangle of weeds, and it was only when she had pushed past the overgrown briars of what must have once been a rose-bed and spied the primroses growing beneath the unpruned suckers that she knew where her work was going to begin.

Half an hour later she had cleared a respectable breathing-space of rich clean soil around the plants. It was still only mid-April and a sharp keen wind whipped her hair into a tangle and stung her skin, but it wasn't the wind that was responsible for the tears now dried to salt on her skin, tears which had seeped relentlessly from her eyes the whole time she was working.

Crying over a man she had known less than a handful of days. She was being ridiculous... diotic, but that didn't stop her whole body tightening in a convulsion of shocked joy when a movement just beyond her vision caught her attention and she turned her head to see Luke walking towards her.

'Sorry about this,' he apologised as soon as he was within speaking distance, 'but something came up, and, of course, without a damned telephone I couldn't get in touch with you to let you know I was going to be late.'

The wind had blown his hair into a similar disorder to hers, ruffling it so that she could see its thick natural curl.

She discovered that she had childishly put her hands behind her back and realised that her gesture had been an instinctive attempt to stop herself from reaching out to touch him.

That alone betrayed how far she had already come down a path she had forbidden herself to tread. She was not a person who reached out easily or naturally to others to touch them. Her childhood had been devoid of that kind of physical contact, and even now, when she was fully adult, she often found herself shrinking back from physical contact with others.

Even more frighteningly, no matter how much she searched her memory she could find no recollection of ever having had that instinctive, automatic reflex need to reach out to Paul the way she has just almost done to Luke, but then she knew already that those feelings she had had for Paul, those feelings she had believed to be the beginnings of love, had been no more than a mild reflection of Paul's own sexual desire for her. She had been flattered by his initial attention and because of that flattery, because of the great need within her to give and receive love, she had deceived herself into thinking she loved him. Her feelings then had grown tentatively, uncertainly and slowly.

What she felt now for Luke was totally different; the emotions she felt towards him had literally burst into life overnight. One moment, or so it seemed, she had had no knowledge of his existence; the next . . . the next he had kissed her, and with that kiss he had either cast a spell on her or touched her so powerfully emotionally that she was now unable to do so much as feel her heart beat without thinking of him.

It made no difference how many times she told herself that she didn't want these feelings; that she was being a fool and worse...that she was going to be hurt. It made no difference how many stern resolutions she made when she was apart from him, as the moment she saw him they were all swept away by the magnetic pull he had on her emotions.

Love at first sight. A ridiculous fairy-tale, a fantasy; impossible to believe in, impossible to trust.

'You've been working hard,' Luke praised.

He bent down to admire the primrose she had revealed and as he did so she caught the scent of his skin, warm and male against the coldness of the fresh air. A wave of dizziness trembled through her, an immediate physical reaction to his nearness that was so acute that it made her heart thunder and her pulses race.

'What made you start here?' he asked her with some amusement as he stood up and surveyed the wilderness all around them.

Logically Melanie supposed that she might more properly have started work at some more organised point, and she flushed a little as she explained to him how the primroses had caught her eye, and how she had felt she must free them from their choking burden of weeds.

'They seemed so...so alone somehow. I wanted to help them, to show them that someone cared.'

Her voice faltered and then stopped as she realised she was making a complete fool of herself, a feeling which was confirmed when Luke said softly, 'Is that why you've been crying? Because you felt sorry for the primroses?'

'I wasn't crying,' she fibbed. 'It was just the wind. I'm not used to living in the country; to being outside; it made my eyes water.'

She might have got away with it if she hadn't started to turn away from him, desperately anxious that he shouldn't make any further comments about her tear-stained face, but even as she moved he was moving too.

One hand on her shoulder, Luke turned her firmly and easily into the warmth of his body while the other cupped her face, his thumb stroking the skin which was stained with her tears.

His scent...that scent which was particularly his was all around her now, dizzying her; bewitching her.

As he lowered his head, he whispered softly against her ear, 'Lucky primroses to have you to shed tears for them and rescue them,' and then his mouth was on her skin, his tongue tenderly licking away the salty traces of her tears.

Her knees felt as though they were about to buckle beneath her. She must have moved, although she had no conscious awareness of having done so, only of being closer to him—so close that she could feel the steady thud of his heart, which was quickly becoming far less steady as his body registered her nearness and reacted to her with such frank maleness that she tensed instinctively. Not in rejection, but perhaps a little in shock. It was still all so new to her; this intimacy which he seemed to take so much for granted; it was still a source of such amazement to her that her closeness could arouse him so quickly and so erotically.

She hadn't spoken, hadn't even tried to break the embrace, but he must have registered that tiny locking of her muscles because his tongue tip stopped its delicious caressing of her skin, and his mouth moved to her ear, where he murmured, 'I'm sorry. I didn't intend that to happen.' As he spoke he eased his body slightly away from hers, but his hand was still cupping her face, and somehow or other the gentle pressure of his fingers was forcing her to look up at him so that he could see right into her eyes.

'The trouble is,' he whispered against her mouth, 'you have an effect on me I find impossible to control. Right now there's nothing I want more than to take you to bed and make love to you.'

Hearing it put so openly into words panicked her. She tried to pull away from him, almost gabbling, 'No...no, I can't...it's...'

'Too soon,' he supplied wryly for her, not, as she had half feared, either taking offence or appearing resentful. 'Yes, I know that, and I also want you to know that I'm not in the habit of behaving like this.'

Both hands were now cupping her face, his thumbs stroking her skin, soothing her jangling nerves, calming her frantic panic, the slow sound of his voice almost mesmeric.

Even so she still managed to tell him shakily, 'That wasn't the impression I got the first time we met.'

He laughed, the corners of his eyes crinkling slightly, amusement curling his mouth, as he teased gently, 'Wasn't it?'

He was looking directly into her eyes. She had no idea what it was he saw there, but suddenly his own expression changed, the amusement dying to be replaced by a sombre, deeper scrutiny that made her nerves tense with a feminine awareness of danger.

'That was different,' he told her huskily. 'Then it was just a game.'

Then? It took her a long time and a lot of courage to ask shakily, 'And now?'

His thumbs were still caressing her skin, but now the sensation wasn't soothing: it was erotic, dangerous, compelling.

'And now it isn't a game any more,' he told her seriously. 'Not for me.'

So this was what it was like to have a craving and to have that craving appeased; this was what it was like to have fasted and then to touch the heights of enhanced awareness; this was what it was like to wake up one day and discover that one's precious dream had turned into reality.

Slowly she raised herself up on her tiptoes and placed her arms around his neck.

As she whispered huskily against his skin, 'And not for me either,' she wondered it he would ever know how much courage it had taken her to utter those words.

'Melanie.'

The way he said her name was like a clarion call of pure rich bells, filled with resonance and joy.

'Look at me,' he commanded, but when she did she discovered that it was his mouth that was immediately within the focus of her eyes, and once she had looked at it and remembered how it had felt against her own she discovered that it was impossible to look away.

She heard Luke say her name again, something between agony and amusement caught in his voice, so that she lifted her gaze to his eyes and then trembled at the brilliance she could see in them.

When he kissed her she responded to him ardently, giving herself to him totally, with all the love she felt for him but was too shy to speak of, and this time when he held her against his body and she felt its hard arousal it wasn't shock that tightened her muscles but pleasure and anticipation.

She felt his hands moving urgently over her body and tensed briefly. In the past when men had tried to caress her with such intimacy she had rejected their caresses, had felt no reciprocal desire for their touch but rather a strong feeling of tension and disquiet—even with Paul, and he had been angry with her too. Yet now, in Luke's embrace, when his hands burrowed beneath her top to stroke the satin smoothness of her bare skin, the *frisson* of sensation she experienced was one of fiercely exciting pleasure and arousal; the need inside her not to immediately put a stop to what he was doing but instead to facilitate his exploration of her body to move against him in deliberate invitation so that his hands gently cupped the soft swell of her breasts.

Heat burned through her, her skin suddenly on fire, suddenly so sensitive and aware that she could actually feel the pulsing hardness of her excited nipples long before Luke's fingers touched them.

When they did, deliberately sliding the silky fabric of her bra free of her skin, she made an involuntary, eager sound of pleasure against his mouth, unable to stop herself from whispering his name, caught as she was between awe and shock.

She had never dreamed it was possible to experience so many wonderful sensations just from one simple caress, and she couldn't help wondering, if just the touch of his hand could make her feel like this, what she would feel when . . . if, if he were actually to caress the same eager tenderness of her breasts with his mouth.

The shudder which convulsed her was felt by them both. It made her tense and open her eyes, her skin flooding with embarrassed hot colour while Luke lifted his mouth from hers and looked down at her.

His eyes held a dazed softness and yet a heat that sent prickles of sensation dancing along her nerve-endings, and when he focused on her, looking first into her eyes and then at her mouth, her heart seemed to do a somersault inside her body.

'You're right,' he told her softly. 'This is neither the time nor the place.'

His hands were still cupping her breasts, and as he spoke he moved the pads of his thumbs gently against her hard nipples, kissing her mouth tenderly, but without passion.

'We'd better go in and get on with that decorating,' he added regretfully, gently easing his hands away from her body, but the metal strap on his watch must have caught on the wool of her sweater because as he moved his arm away from her, her sweater rose up over her body.

Whether it was her own gasp that warned him, or whether he merely chanced to glance down and become aware of what was happening, Melanie had no idea. All she did know was that suddenly Luke seemed to tense, holding them both frozen in an unmoving tableau which had his gaze fixed on the pale nudity of her breasts, their smoothness disturbed by the rash of goose-pimples brought on by a mixture of shock and cold.

She could hear Luke apologising, quickly un-
hooking the pulled thread from his watch-strap,
deftly dealing with it so that her jumper would not
ultimately be damaged, even as he turned his own
body, ensuring that hers was shielded from the
sharpness of the cool breeze, so now it was only
the warmth of the sun that played against her skin,
warming it where it had originally been cold.

As the goose-pimples faded in that warmth,
Melanie discovered several different things; the first
and most shocking surely being the discovery that
not only was there a very definite and very sensual
pleasure to be had in feeling the sun's warmth
against her skin, especially against such an intimate
and sensitive part of her body, but also that there
was something highly erotic and disturbing to her
own sexual self-control in knowing that her body
was so wantonly revealed to Luke's eyes, even if
she herself was not responsible for that situation.

Indeed, as she hurriedly averted her face and
mentally willed Luke to hurry up and complete his
self-imposed task, she found herself acknowledging that it was almost as though her body was actually enjoying flaunting itself before Luke's gaze.

At last she was free, but just as she was about
to restore her clothing to its original order Luke
stopped her, gently taking hold of her hands and
then circling her wrists with fingers that held her
strongly but without any threat or discomfort.

Instinctively she looked down to see what he was
doing, and then blushed rosily at the sight of her
own breasts, their flesh pale and blue-veined, her
nipples in contrast very flushed, very swollen and
erect.

'Luke...' she began to protest, but her voice became a choked sound in her throat as he bent his head and, as though earlier he had read her mind and registered her need, he very slowly started to caress the soft skin between her breasts with his mouth, gradually moving outwards over the gentle swell of her body until at last he reached the sensitive aureole of her breast.

He must at some stage have released her wrists, but she herself had had no awareness of him doing so until she raised her hands to clasp them round his head, and saw that she was free to do so.

Her heart was thudding frantically, her breathing so erratic, so uneven, so shudderingly difficult to accomplish that each breath she took seemed to increase her dizziness and with it her inability to do anything other than to give in to the sensations storming through her.

As Luke drew slowly and sweetly on the taut peak of her breast she heard herself cry out in sensual torment, knew she had curled her fingers into his skin, knew she was behaving with a wantonness that ought to have shocked her, and yet at the same time was powerless to do anything about it other than to make an eager, urgent sound of keening need deep in her throat when Luke slowly lifted his mouth from one breast and then tormentingly repeated the caress against the other.

Quite what would have happened then if they had not been interrupted by the sound of a low-flying plane coming towards them, Melanie had no idea. She only knew that, had he chosen to do so, Luke could quite easily have lain her down here on the damp hard earth and made love to her here among the long tangled grasses, and her body would have welcomed him with eagerness and passion, and that despite the fact that he would have been its first lover.

Even more than the fact that she had been so aroused to desire and need that it had been Luke and not she who had heard the plane first, what shocked her was not that she would have accepted Luke's lovemaking, but that she would have wanted it, invited it, incited and subtly pleaded for it with a hundred feminine messages she had never even known until now that her body was capable of sending.

'Crop dusting,' Luke remarked as she clumsily restored her clothes to order. 'Probably just as well,' he added wryly, and then, turning to her, he looked right into her eyes and added softly, 'I don't know what it is about you, but you have the effect of making me forget everything and everyone else. I think now I can understand...'

When he suddenly stopped speaking, the smile in his eyes wiped away so that they looked coldly bleak, Melanie shivered, feeling chilled and rejected, as though he had withdrawn from her.

'Come on, let's get you inside; you're getting cold.'

His voice was terse, hostile almost. Was that because of her... because of the way she had behaved? Was he shocked, disgusted even, by her wantonness? Was he?

Bleakly she walked towards the house. It seemed impossible to believe now that less than five minutes ago she had been in his arms and that he...

She shivered again.

This was not the way to establish an enduring, committed relationship. This was not the way she had ever envisaged herself behaving. It was alien to her, against all she believed in, against the way she had always lived her life, but when Luke touched her, when he kissed her and held her she seemed to become incapable of using logic and reason; she seemed to become a totally different woman; a woman she herself could barely recognise.

As they walked upstairs together, she paused on the small landing to stare out of the window and into the garden.

Standing behind her, Luke asked her quietly, 'What ultimately do you intend to do with this place? Hang on until all the excitement over the new motorway proposals reach fever pitch and then sell out to the highest bidder?'

Somehow his words had a cynical undertone to them, a bitterness almost that made her frown and turn to face him.

There was so much she felt unable to say to him, so much she must . . . *could* not bring herself to explain. She was afraid that if she told him what she had in mind, he would scoff at her, or even worse deride her; she knew that even Louise would think she was being unworldly and perhaps foolish in her determination to give away her inheritance. Only someone who had suffered as she had, who had lived as she had could truly understand this need she had within herself to pass on to others the gift she had so unexpectedly received.

For her it was enough that she would have this time here; this sense of belonging, of being at one with her environment which came to her so strongly here in the cottage for all its discomfort and lack of modern amenities, but all the time she was conscious of only having the cottage on loan, of holding it in trust for the needs of others, and she had an obligation to those others to see that the cottage and the land realised as much as they could.

There was no real reason why she should not explain all of this to Luke and yet she felt hesitant about doing so, shy almost, so that it was easier somehow to endure the faint condemnation she could see in his eyes, to allow him to think as he so obviously did, that she was being almost over-shrewd; that she was perhaps too money-conscious.

All she could do, then, was to say hesitantly, but honestly, 'A part of me doesn't want to sell. I like living here—in the cottage, I mean, but...'

'But what?' Luke probed.

Melanie looked up at him. She could almost feel the tension emanating from him. He was watching her closely, making her feel acutely self-conscious, almost as though his question was immensely important.

She shrugged the thought aside. He was a detective; asking questions was an important part of his job, which was probably why she felt this awareness of an almost angry urgency behind his question.

But still she couldn't answer it... couldn't explain to him how she felt... couldn't bare her soul to him... was still afraid of his rejection, his contempt.

Even though she had willingly and wantonly bared her body?

She shivered convulsively, shaking her head and turning away from him, saying only, 'I have to sell,' and hoping that Luke would stop questioning her.

* * *

'Well, what do you think of it, now that we're almost finished?'

'*We're* almost finished?' Melanie grinned across at Luke and said apologetically, '*You're* the one who's done all the work. I can't thank you enough, Luke. It looks wonderful. I had no idea it could even begin to look like this.'

The pleasure in her eyes, the way she gestured in helpless admiration and pleasure to the walls surrounding her all betrayed her genuine delight and amazement at the transformation he had wrought.

When Luke had first described to her what he had intended to do, she had only formed a very hazy impression of the finished room, but now that it *was* finished—or virtually—she couldn't help imagining how dull her own meagre efforts would have appeared compared with not just the professionalism of the work Luke had done, but also with his suggestion for changing the entire look of the room.

If she hadn't seen it with her own eyes, Melanie would never have dreamed that something so simple as wallpaper could so drastically alter a room.

The pretty floral paper she had chosen now ran from halfway up the walls, over the ceiling and down the opposite walls where it met the white-painted, newly installed dado rail. Beneath the rail Luke had used a plain toning paper, picking out from her wallpaper the warm peach of the flowers themselves so that now the room did not merely look clean and fresh, but had a very special country charm about it that made her long to press him for his suggestions for the rest of the rooms, and not just for that.

If she was honest with herself she would be forced
to admit that the idea of selling the cottage was
definitely becoming more and more unappealing to
her.

'Something wrong?' Luke asked her, watching
the way she touched the wall behind her with her
fingertips, slowly, lingeringly, almost as though she
was feeling sadness and regret, almost as though...
Angrily he clamped down on his own weakness and
said almost brusquely, 'What you need in here now
is a carpet.'

'A carpet.' Wrenched out of her daydream—of
furnishing this pretty feminine room with some
carefully chosen furniture, of a bed covered in a
soft padded quilt in the same pattern as the paper,
of matching curtains hanging at the windows, with
perhaps pastel bedside lamps and the carpet Luke
had just mentioned—she stared at him for a
moment, knowing how impossible the fulfilment
of such daydreams was.

She would have Louise's furniture, and as for
bedding... Well perhaps she might allow herself
the luxury of buying several yards of fabric and
making a very simple quilt cover. Not the pretty
padded and trimmed variety she would actually
have liked—that would be far too extravagant... and as for carpets... she could perhaps
make do with staining the floorboards, and maybe
if she could find a cheap rug...

The smile she gave Luke was faintly haunted and
sad.

'No...no, I don't think so.'

'My decorating's not good enough to warrant
that kind of expense, is that it?'

Luke had intended the comment to be light-hearted and teasing, but instead it sounded bitter, contemptuous almost.

Melanie's eyes widened, her face flushing as she heard the condemnation in his voice.

The last thing she had wanted to do was to sound self-pitying by letting him know that a new carpet was a luxury she simply could not afford, but she couldn't bear him to think that she wasn't appreciative of all that he had done.

'Oh, no!' she contradicted immediately. 'Luke, your decorating is wonderful...marvellous...I can't get over the difference it's made to this room. I would never have dreamed...' She looked at him shyly and confided, 'It's all so professional and beautiful that it does deserve a new carpet to show it off, but I just can't——' She bit her lip, reluctant even now, even after the time they had spent together, the kisses they had shared, to admit her poverty to him.

The trouble was that although they had shared physical intimacy, although over the last few days they had laughed together, worked together and eaten together, despite the fact that Luke had kept her amused with various stories about his work, despite the fact that he had revealed to her a very astute mind, and an awareness of worldwide issues which pointed to a man who concerned himself very deeply with everything that went on about him, a man of strong views and feelings, a man who was in no way merely the flirtatious lightweight she had first supposed, but someone who was truly concerned for the welfare of his fellow men, she still felt hesitant about confiding fully in him; still felt as though there was some unseen barrier between them, as though, in telling him so much about herself, her thoughts, her feelings, her plans, she was assuming an intimacy, a commitment between them which did not really exist.

He had not, after all, kissed her, or indeed in any way encouraged any intimacy between them since those moments in the garden, and she was beginning to believe that, despite what he had said to her on that occasion, she had over-reacted to him, had imbued his words to her with a seriousness he had never intended and that he, sensing that her emotions were more involved than he would have wanted, had deliberately withdrawn from her and that, as she had originally perceived, all he really wanted from her was a few days' light-hearted flirtation.

'You can't what?' Luke prompted her now. 'You can't afford it?'

Although he said the words lightly, Melanie had an awareness that his tone was in some way assumed to cover a deeper, more intense emotion.

He was avoiding looking at her, Melanie noticed, his body held tensely as though to ward off a physical blow; as though he was waiting for something... but for what? She swallowed painfully. Surely he couldn't think that she expected him to offer to buy the carpet for her? But no; the very suggestion was so preposterous, so diametrically opposed to everything she believed in that she could hardly assimilate the fear that he might actually have made such an assumption.

It was pride; pride and a fear that she might inadvertently have given him exactly such an impression that made her shrug and retort lightly,

'No, it isn't that. It's just that it seems such a waste, when the place is going to be sold anyway.'

'Really? And yet you didn't seem to think that decorating would equally be a waste?'

Again she shrugged, desperately hoping that she was concealing from him how shocked and distressed she was by the antagonism which seemed to have sprung up between them, virtually out of nowhere.

'Originally all I had intended to do was to make the place look a bit cleaner, a bit brighter. I had no intentions of going to the lengths that you——'

'I see. Well, I'm sorry if my interference has led you into unnecessary expense,' she heard him saying acidly. 'You should have said.'

Melanie felt her skin scald with hot colour.

Please stop! she wanted to cry... I don't want this to happen. I don't want to quarrel with you; but it was like stepping on an unsuspected patch of ice—she was on it, she found she was sliding, helpless and totally without any form of control, into very great danger indeed, as though she was someone in a waking nightmare.

She heard herself responding equally coldly and angrily, 'I tried to do so, but you wouldn't listen. After all, it's pointless wasting time on a house that——'

'I quite agree,' Luke interrupted her curtly. 'Oh, and I forgot to tell you, by the way. They came to install my phone late yesterday afternoon, so I shan't need to trouble you for the use of yours from now on.'

While she blinked frantically to hold at bay the weak tears threatening to flood her eyes, and her throat thickened with pain and misery, Melanie heard him adding something about clearing everything away and leaving her in peace.

Peace? Oh, God, didn't he realise what he had done to her and that she would never, ever again know that state of mind? That for the rest of her life she would ache and yearn for him, would need and want him . . . would *love* him?

And yet somehow she managed to keep everything that she was feeling locked away within herself until at last he was gone and she was free to give vent to her emotions, to fling herself headlong on her bed and sob despairingly into her pillow until she had no tears left to cry, until she felt as dry and empty as it was possible for a human being to feel.

CHAPTER SIX

AFTER the way they had parted, Melanie was not totally surprised not to see Luke the following day, nor the one after that; but when three days had gone by without his getting in touch with her she knew that her first assessment of him had been the right one after all, and that for all his tenderness, all his passion, all his whispered words of praise he had only wanted her as a momentary diversion.

At least she had had her bedroom decorated, she told herself cynically, but the truth was that she couldn't even bear to walk inside the room which had initially, if briefly, given her so much pleasure.

She was afraid that just by opening the door and seeing the place where she had spent so much time with Luke she would invite even more heartache than she was already having to endure. And so the bedroom door remained closed, although every time she had to walk past it her heart gave a funny little double beat and the unhappiness engulfing her deepened.

She tried telling herself that it was all for the best; that it was better that their quarrel had precipitated what would inevitably have happened anyway, but, much as her brain was convinced by this logic, her heart refused to listen.

At night she could not sleep, even though she was adopting a deliberate policy of working so hard physically during the daytime that she ought to have fallen deeply asleep the moment her head touched the pillow. *Ought* to have done, but could not, despite the fact that she had scrubbed the house from top to bottom, had moved what pieces of furniture she had, heavy as they were, had meticulously scrubbed out ancient wooden drawers and set them to dry, had scrupulously re-lined those same drawers with odd rolls of wallpaper she had bought at the same time as she had bought some cans of sunny yellow paint with which she intended to brighten up the kitchen, a task which still remained to be tackled since every time she approached those same cans of paint she was reminded unbearably of Luke.

Hot tears would start to sting her eyes, her throat would burn and ache, and such an intensity of pain and anguish would engulf her that she could not bear to start work upon a task which would remind her so poignantly of the time they had spent together.

And so instead she busied herself with other things, with, for instance, on those days when the heavy spring showers kept her inside and out of the garden, cleaning each and every window the house possessed, wiping down the old damaged woodwork, and tried, while she occupied herself with these tasks, to exercise and fill her mind with schemes for redecorating the rooms had she had the ability and the money to do so; and yet, no matter what she did, no matter how hard she strived, it was not just her heart that betrayed her but her mind as well, sneakily causing her to wonder, as she planned a colour scheme or mentally refurnished a room, what Luke's opinion of her plans would be, or what Luke would think of what she was doing, or what advice Luke would give her, were he there to help her.

Only Luke wasn't there, and the sooner she accepted that fact and taught herself to forget him and everything he had come to mean to her the faster she would learn to come to terms with her heartache.

Because coming to terms with it, accepting that the burden of her love for Luke was something she would carry with her for the remainder of her life, was going to be the best she could manage to do.

There was no question of her ever truly getting over him, of her ever being able to cast him right out of her heart, of her being able to forget that he had ever existed.

In time, surely, the sharpness of her present pain would dim; in time she might find that just to recall a specific turn of his head, a note in his voice, the way he had smiled at her would not cause such a red-hot pain to knife so sharply through her that she found she could scarcely breathe for the intensity of it. In time.

But for now all she could do was to endure and go on enduring—something she was surely accomplished in doing. The acceptance of emotional pain was something she had learned a long time ago, something that was as much a part of her personality as her honesty and her vulnerability.

On fine days Melanie worked out in the garden, not on the patch near the roses which she had originally been clearing. She had found she could scarcely even bear to walk past that small area. She had not even been able to clear away the weeds she had pulled out and found that when she did have to walk past the spot where Luke had kissed her, had touched her, she had to avert her face in case she became rooted to the spot, unable to move away, unable to do anything other than stand there while tears of pain and rejection poured down her face.

Instead she was working on what had once been a vegetable plot. On its periphery were the remnants of gooseberry and redcurrant bushes, and she had accidentally unearthed a couple of clumps of rhubarb, amazingly growing healthily despite their choking cloak of weeds.

She had promised herself that she would pick that same rhubarb and make an excellent pie, but in spite of this the rhubarb remained unpicked, perhaps because the thought of going to all that trouble just for herself seemed pointless, or perhaps because her appetite had decreased so sharply, so much so that the unexpected sight of herself in an old-fashioned pierglass in one of the spare bedrooms shocked her into realising how much weight she must have lost.

Was that really her, she wondered uncertainly, that drawn, wan creature with the pale face and huge eyes, clad in jeans which looked as though they were at least a couple of sizes too big?

Halfway through the week she was brought forcibly into an awareness of just how damaging her brief relationship with Luke had been when Louise's husband, Simon, called with the furniture Louise had promised her.

Louise had already telephoned to warn her that he was on his way, adding that she would not be able to come with him, but that she hoped to come and see her soon.

'How's the decorating going?' she had enquired, and when Melanie had replied abstractedly that it was finished, she had queried softly, 'And the decorator?'

The same answer pertained to that question as well, but Melanie could not bring herself to give it. Instead she said as casually as she could, 'Oh, Luke? I haven't seen him since the bedroom was finished. He's got his own phone now.'

And she was grateful to Louise for not pressing the matter, even while it hurt her to sense that her friend had probably guessed without needing to be told just how much Luke was coming to mean to her.

'And you still intend to sell up?'

'Yes. There's a rumour in the village that the verdict on the motorway extension is going to be brought forward a few weeks.'

'Well, let's keep our fingers crossed that it is going ahead,' Louise told her. 'That way you're bound to get an awful lot more for the property.'

'Yes,' Melanie agreed, but she knew she sounded less enthusiastic than she should. She had tried telling herself that it was her duty to ensure that she could get as much from the sale as she could, but with each day that passed she found herself growing more and more reluctant to part with the cottage, even to the extent of sometimes actually falling into the idiotic and painful daydream of actually living here with Luke, of the house, clean and warm and filled with the sound of their children's laughter, with happiness and sunshine, of the garden bearing signs of family activities, its jungle tamed to give way to soft country borders and the lawn, while shorn and green, bearing the unmistakable prints of small feet.

That these daydreams were the utmost folly she needed no one to tell her; that they were self-destructive and painful, that they were actually stopping her from putting Luke out of her mind and trying to get on with her life she also knew, but no matter how hard she tried, no matter how determined she was not to allow herself to fall into the trap of permitting them, they seemed to creep up on her, catching her when she was weak and vulnerable, calling to her with all the hypnotic allure of a siren's song, promising her delight but in reality giving her nothing but pain and reinforcing what she already knew: that Luke did not want her.

After Louise's warning telephone call, Melanie stayed as close as she could to the front of the house so that she would be in earshot of Simon's arrival.

The lane that ran past her house was seldom used by others, the traffic on it reduced to the odd farm vehicle and people toing and froing between the two farms which lay beyond the cottage.

A faint, depressing drizzle had kept her inside virtually all morning. In her desire to wipe Luke completely from her mind she had cleaned the house so thoroughly that there was virtually no cleaning now left for her to do. Only the redecorating. However, every time she looked at the cans of paint she could think only of Luke and the bedroom upstairs into which she could not bring herself to walk, and a wave of aloneness so acute that it was a real physical pain swept over her.

And, besides, what was the point of spending time and money on the cottage when at the end of the day she was not going to be living here, was not going to be able to enjoy the fruits of her own labours?

The truth was that she was afraid of spending too much time working on the place because of the possibility of becoming too attached to it, that when

the time came she would not be able to bring herself
to part with it.

Above the bedrooms ran a long attic into which
Melanie had not as yet ventured, and which could
be reached via a trap-door in her own room.

However, to get into the attic she would need a
pair of stepladders: the stepladders which she had
carried downstairs and stowed away in the garage
when Luke had finished the decorating.

She hesitated before going to get them, wishing
that Simon would arrive and so give her something
to busy herself with.

Whereas once she had enjoyed her solitude and
having time to herself, now she found that she
dreaded it—dreaded it because she was terrified that
she would fall into the too tempting trap of allowing her mind to dwell on Luke.

To think and to remember; to daydream. If only
it would stop raining she could go out and work in
the garden. As she paused, hesitating, she thought
she heard the sound of a vehicle lumbering down
the lane.

Warning herself that it might only be one of the
farm tractors, she hurried outside, relief filling her
as she recognised the driver of the bulky hired van.

'I've brought Alan with me. I hope you don't
mind,' Louise's husband apologised after he had
stopped the van and Melanie had welcomed him,
'only this old furniture is a bit bulky and heavy and
I didn't fancy my chances of getting it up your stairs
on my own.'

'Of course I don't mind,' Melanie assured him.
'In fact I'm very grateful to you both. You must
be hungry, though. How about some lunch before
you start unloading?'

'Great idea,' Simon approved.

Melanie grinned at him. She knew from Louise that he had a hearty appetite. Louise was always threatening to put him on a diet, although for all his enjoyment of good food he was not a man who was unpleasantly overweight; rather perhaps a touch more solidly built that he should have been. Even so, Melanie thought that it suited him. He had about him the air of a man who was content with his life. Melanie found him relaxing and good company. He was kind to her in a slightly avuncular and totally non-threatening way, which she liked. That he also tended to be rather protective was something which, while previously unfamiliar to her, she had discovered gave her a warm, cared-for feeling.

Alan, she learned over the lunch she had prepared for the two men, was a long-standing friend of Simon's, although, unlike him, he wasn't married.

'At least not now,' he told Melanie rather wryly after praising her homemade *potage bonne femme*. 'I used to work away from home on long contracts abroad. I suppose I can't blame Moira for getting fed up with it, and with me. I tried to tell her that I was doing it for her and for the kids, and she certainly never complained about the money I was making.' He pulled a face, his voice heavy with a cynicism that failed to mask his pain as he added, 'What I didn't bargain for was returning from one of these contracts to discover that she'd got herself a new life and a new man; that she was leaving me and taking my kids with her, claiming that I wasn't a good father to them or a good husband to her because I was never there.'

Melanie bit her lip, feeling both sorry for him and sad at the break-up of his marriage, even though she suspected that there must be a great deal more to it than merely the fact that he had had to work away from home.

'Marriage—you can keep it,' he concluded bitterly. 'From now on I'm going all out for Number One, putting myself first. Do you know, the last time I saw my kids, the boy—*my* son—actually referred to this other guy as "dad"?'

'Come on,' Simon intervened. 'We'd better make a start on shifting this furniture, otherwise it will never get done. You leave everything to us,' he told Melanie cheerfully. 'I'll just take a look at the stairs first though. Which room do you want this stuff in, Mel?'

'The first one on the left at the top of the stairs, please,' Melanie told him.

It was the room in which she herself was sleeping. What she intended to do was to move out the existing furniture and reorganise the room around her unexpected presents. What she would have liked to have done was to put the oak furniture in the newly decorated bedroom, preferably on top of a newly fitted carpet. If she closed her eyes she could just see it now: the heavy traditional furniture, so deplored by Louise, would look good against her new décor, and would fit in admirably with the oddly sloping walls and generally old-fashioned air of the pretty bedroom; but once she did that, once the room was furnished, it would be far too tempting to move into it herself and if she did that her dreams would never be free of Luke. Never.

She was already suffering enough during the day without having her nights tormented by him as well.

Guiltily she acknowledged that it had been foolish of her to give in to the whim of staining and sealing the scrubbed floorboards, and of buying that sheepskin rug she just hadn't been able to resist on her last trip to Knutsford to stock up on food. True, a really good-quality plain carpet in the same shade of peach as the lower half of the walls would have looked even better than her stained floorboards, and certainly would have felt far more luxurious, but, since she didn't intend to use the room, since she had never intended to do anything with the house than simply clean and tidy it up a little, and since she had certainly never intended to allow it to get so firm a grip on her heart, it was pointless allowing herself to imagine what it would feel like to push back the bedclothes and to step out of bed on to the thick luxuriousness of a soft warm carpet. Just as it was an even greater folly to wonder what it would be like if Luke was sharing the room with her, sharing the bed with her, if she and Luke——

'Penny for them,' Simon teased her, causing her to flush brilliantly and bite down on her bottom lip.

'They aren't worth it,' she told him bravely, unaware of the concern and compassion which touched his eyes as he looked at her down-bent head.

In the end, she took Louise's advice and left the men to their self-appointed task, promising them a cup of tea and a slice of the cake she had made the previous evening once they had finished.

There seemed to be an awful lot of banging and crashing noises, accompanied by several rather salty curses, but eventually they both returned downstairs, and Simon told her triumphantly, 'There; it's all upstairs and reassembled, although I'm sure my back will never be the same again. That bed-frame——'

'Bed-frame?' Melanie queried. Louise had not mentioned a bed-frame.

'Yes, it was upstairs in our loft, and Louise said that as you were having the rest of the suite you might as well have that as well. By the way,' he added with a grin, 'has anyone told you before that don't seem to be able to tell left from right? We guessed you'd got it wrong when we opened the door of the bedroom on the left and found it was already furnished, especially when we realised that the room opposite it was empty and quite obviously ready and waiting for the furniture. Louise has the same problem. She drives me mad at times!'

Melanie couldn't say a word. They had put the furniture in the empty room...in the room she had sworn she would keep closed and empty until the house was safely sold, just so that she wouldn't have to walk into it and be reminded of Luke.

Common sense told her that just because the room was now furnished didn't mean that she had to use it, that she could just as easily close the door on it now as she had done before, but she had an uneasy, despairing suspicion that she wouldn't be able to resist the temptation of opening the door and seeing just how the room looked with the addition of some traditional furniture, a suspicion which was confirmed when Simon asked her cheerfully, 'Well, aren't you going to come up and see how it looks?'

'I...' What could she say? If she refused, both men would think it odd and that she was ungrateful, and they had worked very hard...

'Well, yes...I...'

'Come on, then. I must admit, it looks surprisingly good in there—much better than it did in our place. Of course this house is a lot older. I like the way you've decorated it, by the way. Just wait until I tell Louise; she'll be over here like a shot, wanting to see what you've done. It seems a shame to have to sell it when you're putting in so much hard work, but then I suppose it is too large for one person and too far out to be really practical, although it's less than an hour's drive from Chester,' he mused, unconsciously repeating one of Luke's comments to her.

Luke. Her hand was on the knob of the bedroom door, turning it and pushing the door open, her brain momentarily cheating and deceiving her so that as she turned towards the window it was almost as though a shadow moved inside the room.

Luke. His name was virtually on her lips before she silenced it, wondering with horror what on earth the two men would have thought if they had heard her calling out to someone who wasn't there.

'Mm. Your decorating friend has made a good job of this.' Simon approved, touching the paintwork of the dado rail, thankfully oblivious to the tension which was gripping her as she walked into the room.

A double bed now faced her as she stood just inside the door, a large, heavy wardrobe on the wall opposite it. The two men had placed the dressing-table in front of the window and the man's dressing-chest on the wall at right-angles to it.

Whereas before the room had looked newly decorated, now suddenly it seemed to have a more
homely, settled air to it, now it was possible to imagine curtains at the window and the duvet cover
on the bed, a bed which, she noticed, was accompanied by what looked suspiciously like a brand
new mattress.

When she said as much, rather accusingly, to
Simon, he flushed a little uncomfortably and said
defensively, 'It was Louise's idea. It was one we
bought last year, and then found out too late that
it wasn't suitable for my back. It wasn't any use to
us and Louise said that you might as well have it;
that a furnished house always sells better than an
empty one.'

There was nothing Melanie could say. To refuse
to accept this additional gift would be ungrateful
and possibly even hurtful to Louise, who had so
kind-heartedly and thoughtfully given it to her.
Even as she contemplated offering to pay for it, she
knew that such an offer would immediately be
spurned. Perhaps instead she could take Louise and
Simon and even Alan out for a meal to show her
gratitude for all that they had done. Perhaps that
might be an idea; she could ring Louise when the
two men had left, to thank her for her extra gift
and to suggest such an invitation.

After she had thanked them and made them
another cup of tea, the two men were ready to leave.
Melanie accompanied them out to the van, and
while Alan climbed into the driver's side Simon
turned to her, taking her in his arms to give her a
warm hug.

Just as he did so, a huge BMW swept down the
lane towards them, the sound of its approach start-

ling them both since it was being driven far too fast
on such a quiet country lane.

As far as Melanie could see, the car had only two
occupants—a grey-haired man in his late fifties who
gave her a hard, thin-lipped look which for some
reason made her go cold inside and cling anxiously
to Simon's comforting shoulder. The other oc-
cupant of the car was a young woman, perhaps
three or four years Melanie's senior; her relationship to the older man was obvious from the features she shared with him, although where his hair
was grey hers was strikingly coal-black and very
expensively styled.

She too seemed to stare at Melanie with more
than merely casual curiosity, although the dislike
and malice in her gaze was spiked with a very obvious satisfaction.

'Pleasant-looking pair, weren't they?' Simon
commented when they had driven past. 'Know
them, do you?'

'No,' Melanie answered him honestly. 'I've never
seen either of them before.'

'Mm. Well, they were certainly interested in you.
Perhaps they've heard that you're putting the place
up for sale and were prospective buyers, although
neither of them looked the type to choose to live
in such an isolated spot. I see the pair of them enjoying and needing a far more high-profile kind of
lifestyle, and there's probably plenty of money to
support it.'

As she listened to Simon, Melanie recalled that
Louise had often remarked that her husband could
be very astute when it came to summing up others,
and just before he gave her a final hug and then
released her to climb into the passenger seat of the

van, he commented warningly, 'Watch it where that pair's concerned, young Mel. From the looks they were giving you, neither of them struck me as feeling particularly friendly towards you. Are you sure you don't know them?' She shook her head, and then wrapped her arms around her body as though already warding off some kind of threat.

It was still drizzling, the grass at her feet so wet that the damp was soaking through her shoes. As she watched the van disappear down the muddy lane, she stared disconsolately after it.

For the first time since she had moved into the cottage she felt alone in a way that frightened her.

After so much institutionalised living, she had just begun to discover how much she actually enjoyed living on her own, how much freedom it gave her. So far she had slept at night in the cottage completely alone without feeling the slightest qualm; but now, whether because of the way the two in the car had looked at her or because of Simon's warning, she experienced a sense of foreboding, of reluctance to go back inside almost.

Which was utterly ridiculous. After all, what did she have to fear from two complete strangers?

Melanie stared at the garden. She wished it was dry enough for her to do some work outside, to dissipate her odd mood with hard physical labour, to dispel the sensation of being cut off from the rest of the world, a sensation emphasised by the mistiness that was now permeating the landscape, brought on by the damp and the drizzle.

When she walked into the cottage the phone was ringing. As she rushed to pick up the receiver a thrill of sensation raced through her. Without even thinking of checking it, she held her breath, aching to hear Luke's voice at the other end of the line, but instead the voice she did hear was the dry pedantic one of the solicitor.

'Ah, Miss Foden,' he began formally. 'You may remember that some little time ago you got in touch with me concerning a conversation you had had with a Mr Hewitson regarding his desire to purchase the cottage and its land. You were concerned at the time that some prior verbal agreement to such a sale might have existed between my late client and Mr Hewitson and I was able to advise you that this was not the case.'

Disappointment had formed a giant lump in her throat and an aching pain around her heart. Swallowing hard, she tried to focus on what the solicitor was saying to her.

'Has something occurred to alter that advice?' she asked him seriously, not sure where his conversation was leading.

'Not at all,' he told her. 'However, Mr Hewitson's legal advisers have been in touch with me with an offer for the purchase of the land and the cottage, which, as they point out, should the new motorway extension be diverted to the secondary proposed route, would be very generous indeed.'

He paused, and Melanie swallowed again. 'I see. So, are you recommending me to accept this offer?'

'Well, without the benefit of the new motorway extension to boost local land values, the offer is indeed a good one, more than you could hope to realise from an auction of the cottage and the land as they stand. However, should the extension go ahead the offer comes nowhere near the true value that the land would then have.

'I cannot advise you as to your decision, my dear. That must be yours and yours alone.'

Melanie hesitated. If she sold out to David Hewitson now he would tear down the cottage; he would cover the land with small, box-like houses without character or beauty, and a home which had been in her benefactor's family for many generations would be gone forever. She had already been told by the solicitor that her benefactor had consistently refused to sell out to the builder. Even if by doing so she could make more money for charity, she felt obligated to take into consideration her benefactor's views and feelings. The mere fact that he had refused during his own lifetime to sell out to the builder told its own story.

She paused and then said huskily, 'I can't agree to sell to Mr Hewitson. I—I don't feel it would be what Mr Burrows would have wanted. I think he would have preferred to see someone...a family living here in the cottage. After all, it was his home for so long.'

'Yes, indeed,' the solicitor agreed. 'But you must realise, my dear, that whoever you eventually sell to might not share that view, and could quite easily decide to dispose of the property by selling it to Mr Hewitson.'

It was a possibility that had not occurred to her before, but now that it was pointed out to her she realised how naïve she had been.

She wondered frantically if there was any way in which she could stipulate that any purchaser could not destroy the cottage, and then told herself shakily that she was being overly sentimental and could not have her cake and eat it.

After all, the only real way to ensure that the cottage stayed intact was to live in it herself, but in order to do that she would have to break the promise she had made to herself and to her unknown benefactor that his gift to her would be used to benefit others and not just herself.

'Would you like some time to think things over?' the solicitor asked her kindly.

Immediately Melanie shook her head and then, realising that he couldn't see her, said quickly, 'No...no...I don't need any time. I—I'm not going to accept any offer Mr Hewitson makes.' Inwardly she was acknowledging that the only real way of protecting the cottage, short of making it her permanent home, which she could not do, would be to pray that the powers that be changed their collective minds and adopted the second choice for the route of the new motorway extension; that way the cottage would be safe from men like Hewitson.

'Very well, then, I'll convey your decision to Mr Hewitson's legal advisers.'

There was a small pause, and then he added cautioningly, 'I should perhaps warn you that Mr Hewitson is a very aggressive and hot-tempered man, a man who isn't used to not getting his own way.'

As she thanked her solicitor for his warning and replaced the receiver, Melanie wondered tiredly why she was being subjected to so much misfortune. She would, she decided wearily, have a hot bath and an early night.

After all, what was there to stay up for? She was growing weary of her own company, of spending evening after evening despairingly reliving every second, every heartbeat of the brief space of time she had spent with Luke. And to what purpose? All she was doing was simply torturing herself, causing herself additional pain and misery.

At nine o'clock she locked the doors and went upstairs to bed, but it seemed that the day wasn't finished with her yet and had still one more trial in store for her.

As she climbed into bed there was an ominous cracking sound and even as her body tensed the bed suddenly tilted to one side, causing her to roll on to the floor.

Grimly inspecting the damage, she discovered that her brand new bed must have had a weakness in the frame, and that the too soft cheap wood had given way beneath the strain of the mattress.

Even to her inexperienced eyes it was obvious that there was no way it could be repaired, never mind made usable for the rest of the night.

Which left her with two options. Either she could use the new bed Louise had so kindly given her and sleep in the bedroom which she and Luke had decorated together and suffer the consequences of doing so, or, alternatively, she could sleep in the bed which had originally belonged to John Burrows. As she bit her lip she acknowledged that she was probably being overly sensitive, but she still could not bring herself to sleep in that particular bed.

Which meant it would have to be the newly decorated spare room, where she would probably spend the night tormented by memories and dreams of Luke.

As she miserably gathered her things together, telling herself that for tonight she would simply have to use her pillow and wrap herself in her quilt since

she had no suitable double-bed-sized sheets or
bedding, she prayed that the fates would quickly
grow tired of tormenting someone who could surely
only provide them with minimal sport, and leave
her on her own to deal with her unhappiness and
despair as best she could.

CHAPTER SEVEN

IN THE morning it seemed as though Melanie's prayers had been answered, for not only had she slept deeply and well but the sun was shining, which meant that she would be able to get out of the house and into the garden.

Even so, she felt wearily lethargic as she washed and dressed, reluctant to face the day, reluctant to face life, she acknowledged as she sipped unenthusiastically at her coffee and pushed a piece of untasted toast around her plate.

The last thing she felt like doing was eating, but only this morning as she had climbed out of bed she had experienced a return of the warning dizziness which had been such an unpleasant feature of her bout of flu. Her doctor had warned her then not to overdo things, to eat properly and to rest as much as she could, and she was guiltily aware that over the last few days she had not merely completely ignored this advice but had done exactly the opposite, neglecting to eat and finding it impossible to rest.

This morning, however, that slight dizziness and the breathlessness which had accompanied it as she'd come downstairs had reminded her of how ill she had been.

A morning spent working outside in the fresh air would do her good, she told herself sturdily. It would restore her appetite and, if she was lucky, make her feel so tired that she simply would not have the energy to think about Luke.

As soon as she had cleared away her breakfast things, she went back upstairs and changed into the practical pair of cotton overalls she had bought in Knutsford. Not only were they made from service-able and sensible cotton, but they were an at-tractive shade of soft green. It was true that they were rather large for her small frame but, once the legs were tucked securely into her wellington boots, she felt that she presented a very workwomanlike appearance indeed.

Outside the grass was still very wet from the pre-vious day's rain, the ground inclined to be muddy and slippery.

Melanie headed straight for the vegetable patch she was trying to reclaim, biting her lip hard as she had to walk past the spot where Luke had kissed her and caressed her so intimately, so tenderly—so lovingly, she had stupidly thought—until he had turned away from her and she had realised that she was simply deluding herself, that what he felt for her was nothing more than mere male desire, im-personal and fleeting.

Stop it, she warned herself as her thoughts threatened to get out of hand. There was little point in deliberately causing herself more misery.

The garage had revealed a good supply of garden tools and if they were inclined to be rather heavy for her, well, at least they were saving her money.

Even so, as she busied herself in trying to remove the stubborn weeds from the ground she found herself wishing she had a fork that was a little less unwieldy, something designed for a woman to use and not for a man.

The patch of ground she was trying to clear must at some stage have produced summer salad vegetables, because as she dug she was unearthing the remains of what would have once been metal cloches and the soil was full of splintered pieces of glass.

Melanie knew from her reading that modern gardeners used polythene instead of glass, and had already decided that when the time was right and provided she had cleared enough space she would try her hand at producing her own lettuces; but now that day seemed a long way off, and she grimaced in disgust as her fork hit yet another buried obstacle. This time the piece of glass she unearthed was quite large, but jaggedly and dangerously broken.

As she placed it cautiously in the old-fashioned wheelbarrow she had found in the garage, she was glad of the gardening gloves she had extravagantly bought.

After an hour of strenuous digging, during which she had covered little more than a few yards, Melanie was forced to acknowledge that the task of clearing the vegetable-bed was going to prove much harder than she had envisaged. Her daydreams of beautiful, healthy green rows of growing crops had slowly faded, disappearing beneath the hard reality of the clogging soil sticking so determinedly to her fork, and the mass of broken glass which lay beneath the surface.

It would take a team of dedicated, hard-working men weeks to clear this one small patch, she thought despairingly. Already her back was aching, her muscles tightening in rebellious dislike of the work she was enforcing on them.

There was a hollow sickly feeling inside her stomach which warned her that it was time she had something to eat, but a stubborn grittiness she must have inherited from one of her unknown antecedents forced her to keep going, even though her body was trying its best to tell her that she needed to eat and rest.

Forced to pause in her exertions, she lifted a tired hand to her hair, pushing it out of the way. As she did so she saw Luke walking down the garden towards her.

Shock and panic exploded inside her. She had a foolhardy impulse to throw down the fork and run away from him, but she managed to quell it, managed to force her trembling mouth to form a weak imitation of a coolly polite smile—the kind of smile she would have given a stranger.

As he came nearer, she could see that he was frowning. Now that she was over the first stomach-churning shock of disbelief that he was actually here, her heart was beating shallowly and rapidly, her whole body registering the effect his presence was having on her.

She could feel her skin starting to burn; could feel the trembling start low down in her body and gradually creep through her muscles, so that she was obliged to turn away from him and start digging again to prevent him from seeing what was happening to her.

Totally unable to concentrate on what she was doing, she struck the fork blindly into the soil, using far too much force, so that when it struck sharply against something just beneath the surface she was putting so much weight on the shaft of the fork that she lost her balance, her feet sliding forward in the sticky mud.

As she fell she heard Luke's warning shout, but it was already too late: she couldn't do a thing to save herself.

She saw the wickedly dangerous piece of glass protruding from the earth, had a sickening fore-knowledge of what was going to happen, and yet could do nothing to protect herself as she fell against it and felt the sharp broken point of it tear through her overalls and rip against the vulnerable flesh of her thigh.

As she cried out she was vaguely aware of Luke reaching for her, lifting her, cursing under his breath as he picked her up bodily and set off towards the house.

As he balanced her against his body while he opened the kitchen door, she heard him saying grimly, 'I just hope to God you've had the sense to keep your tetanus injections up to date.'

As she tried to tell him that she had, she made the mistake of looking down at her leg. The green fabric of her overalls was jaggedly torn, but what caused her to tremble and close her eyes was not the sight of her ripped clothes, but the quickly growing bright scarlet stain dyeing the fabric as blood flowed from the cut in her thigh.

Melanie had never considered herself particu-larly squeamish, but suddenly the sight of so much blood—her own blood—made her feel acutely nauseous and for some reason very cold.

She heard Luke demanding roughly, as he carried her towards the stairs, 'Tetanus injections, Melanie; *are* they up to date?' and just managed to nod her head in confirmation that they were before the coldness engulfing her became mind-numbing, stealing her consciousness away.

She came round briefly to discover that she was lying half-naked on the bathroom floor, that Luke had raided her medicine cupboard to find a pair of scissors with which he had ruthlessly cut away her overalls, and that he was now leaning over her, carefully cleaning the wound in her leg.

She still felt terribly cold, and her leg was beginning to ache and throb. She started to protest at what Luke was doing, trying to tell him that she could manage for herself even while common sense told her that she could not; but, as she struggled to sit up and command his attention, he told her grimly, without turning his head, 'Don't move, Melanie. I'm not sure how deep this damned thing is. I don't think it's too bad, although it's still bleeding heavily.'

As she gave a wrenching shudder, he turned to look at her and told her bluntly, 'You're damned lucky you didn't sever an artery. What possessed you to go on digging there, when you must have seen that it was littered with broken glass?'

The shock—or was it the loss of blood?—was making her feel quite light-headed. Indignantly she told him, 'I was quite safe until you appeared.'

'So, it's my fault, is it?'

She knew that her accusation was probably unjust, but she was too proud and too stubborn to take the words back. For what seemed like a long time they simply looked at one another. He looked different, somehow, Melanie realised: older... tireder... harder in some indefinable way.

'There's really no need for you to do this——'
she began to tell him, but he stopped her and said
curtly,

'I need to check that there isn't any glass
embedded in your skin. I don't think there is...
This will probably hurt,' he warned her as he turned
his back on her and, after disinfecting his hands,
started to probe the jagged flesh.

It did hurt, so much so that she had to bite down
hard on her bottom lip to stop herself from crying
out.

As she felt the weakness inside her start to spread,
she told herself that she was not going to faint
again, that she *was* going to stay conscious and tell
Luke to go, that she *didn't* need any help from him,
and somehow or other she managed to stay conscious while he meticulously inspected the wound
and then, having pronounced himself satisfied that
it was free of any splinters of broken glass, started
to clean it all over again.

The cut was still bleeding freely, but, even though
Melanie knew it would be wiser not to look at what
Luke was doing and to either turn her head away
or close her eyes, the contained, deft movement of
his hands, his skin alien and male against the pale
softness of her own thigh, had such a mesmeric
effect upon her that she simply could not stop
herself from following their every movement.

Perhaps it was the fluid with which he was
cleaning the wound that made the blood seem to
flow so freely and so copiously; perhaps it was the
fact that she hadn't been eating properly that made
her feel so light-headed and dizzy; perhaps it was
because she was lying on the bathroom floor
wearing nothing other than her bra, panties and

socks that was making her feel so cold; she had no idea. What she *did* know was that the combination of cold, weakness and nausea was swiftly making it harder and harder for her to hang on to full consciousness and that, as hard as she battled to hold on to it, she was no match for the insidious, swiftly running, numbing tide of cold that was sweeping up through her body.

When she couldn't fight it any longer, she made a small sound of despair that caused Luke to turn his head and look briefly at her.

It was probably just as well that she had fainted, he reflected tiredly. The cut was deep and she had been very lucky indeed not to sustain as far more serious injury, but once her thigh was securely bandaged the bleeding would slow down and stop. He suddenly felt very old—very drained. His mouth compressed.

Although she was vaguely conscious of what Luke was doing, it wasn't until he had picked her up and carried her first into the bedroom she had been using and then into the newly decorated one into which she had moved the previous night that she actually came round properly.

She tried to demur as he pushed back the duvet and placed her on the bed, but Luke was ignoring her, carefully wrapping the quilt round her before telling her tersely, 'I'm going downstairs now to make you something to drink and something to eat. What on earth have you been doing to yourself? And don't, for God's sake, tell me that you don't eat because you can't afford to.'

Helplessly Melanie stared after him as he strode towards the door. The cutting voice in which he had delivered that final comment had hurt, and when she closed her eyes in mute despair she wasn't sure if it was the pain in her thigh or the pain in her heart that caused the tears she was desperately trying to suppress.

All she really wanted now was for Luke to go and leave her in peace. How could she have been so stupid as to have had that accident? If Luke had not been there to help her... She shuddered inwardly. It was no use telling herself that if Luke *hadn't* been there the accident would not have occurred in the first place. She could not be sure enough of that to convince herself it was the truth, even if she had hurled just such an accusation at Luke.

As she lay shivering beneath the duvet, frightening images danced behind her closed eyelids. What if that spike of glass had pierced an artery? What if she had not taken Louise's advice and made sure that her tetanus injections were up to date before moving to the country? What if...?

Her teeth started to chatter so loudly as shock set in that she did not hear Luke return, until the sharp hiss of the breath he exhaled when he saw the state she was in alerted her to his presence. She opened her eyes, her heart jerking as though it were on a string like a yo-yo.

Luke was carrying a tray, which he put down on the oak chest of drawers. It held an omelette on a plate, the sight of which made Melanie's stomach churn even more nauseatingly, and what looked like a mug of coffee.

'What is it? What's wrong?' Luke demanded as he approached the bed.

'I feel so cold,' Melanie told him shakily.

'Cold?'

To her consternation, he sat down beside her, casually sliding his hand beneath the duvet and placing it against her bare skin. The warmth made her shiver even harder and long to creep closer to him so that she could absorb the heat of his body. It was an instinctive, totally non-sexual need, but one which nevertheless made her tense in rejection of her own feelings.

'You've lost quite a lot of blood,' she heard Luke saying. He was frowning as he looked down at her. 'Perhaps I should call a doctor, just . . .'

Immediately Melanie shook her head. 'No, no, there's no need for that. I'm OK, really.'

'Are you?'

The brooding look her gave her made her focus on his face. He looked oddly gaunt and tense, and she had to quell an impulse to reach out and touch him.

'Well, I wish I could say the same thing,' he told her roughly, adding quickly in an impassioned voice, 'My God, do you realise how close you came to——?' He broke off and swallowed, a small muscle jerking under the smooth flesh of his jaw as he clenched his teeth and swore huskily. 'Hell, Melanie, don't you ever dare do anything like this to me again. You've knocked at least ten years off my life and I . . .'

His voice became completely suspended. Melanie's eyes widened with shock and awareness of the emotions he seemed unable to control. Was this really Luke, the same Luke who had virtually walked out on her, now gazing at her with what looked suspiciously like tears in his eyes, his fingers clenching and unclenching where he was gripping her arm?

'Melanie, I've missed you so damned much.'

She wasn't sure which of them moved first, but suddenly she was in his arms, her own wrapping around him as he buried his face in the soft skin of her throat, his voice muffled as he told her, 'When I saw you fall on to that glass I...'

He gave a violent shudder, his lips searching convulsively for the pulse of the life force beating in her throat. The sensation of the moist heat of his mouth against her skin sent bolt after bolt of unbearable reaction shooting through her body.

Her nausea, her weakness, her determination to expel him from her life were all forgotten as she clung dizzily to him, knowing with some deep female instinct that, no matter how fierce and elemental his passion might become in the aftermath of his shock, it would still be tempered by tenderness; that, no matter how intense his need to possess her might be, it would never turn to selfish greed; that in fact, no matter how savage the storm that swept them both might be, he would still keep her safe.

Quite how she knew these things was beyond logic or reason; it was a soul-deep knowing; an instinctive awareness; something she could not challenge no matter how much caution might try to urge her to resist the fierce pull of both his and her own growing desire.

Once it would have shamed and shocked her to know that she could feel this way; that a man, especially this man, simply had to touch her for all her resolutions to forget him to vanish like early morning mist in the heat of the sunlight.

But not now. Not now, with Luke tugging away the duvet that separated their bodies, his hands trembling betrayingly, while his mouth continued to plunder the soft skin of her throat and the heat of his body, even through his clothes, burned hers as though it had been exposed to a direct flame.

'Melanie, if I'd lost you . . .'

She could almost feel the emotion in the tortured words he stifled against her skin. Beneath her palm, his heart was racing fiercely, pounding its message of desire and urgency into her own flesh until she could feel its echo right through her body.

When his hands moved gently over her body to remove what was left of her clothing she moved eagerly to assist him, and then watched, wide-eyed and dry-mouthed, as he then removed his own with a lot more haste and a lot less care.

Once she would have been embarrassed, ashamed even, of her own nudity, and certainly she would have felt alarmed and threatened by his; but now it was awe and delight that made her catch her breath at the sight of his maleness, that made her ache to reach out and touch him, to stroke her fingertips over his skin and feel if it was as satiny and hot as it looked.

Wonderingly she studied the flesh that lay over muscles and bones so different from her own, her fascinated gaze travelling the length and then the breadth of the male body so close to hers.

Where her body was soft and curved, Luke's was taut and hard, the flesh drawn sleekly over the underlying muscles. Where her skin was smooth and delicate, his was rough with the growth of dark hair that her fingers itched to touch to discover if it felt as vibrant with life as it looked. As her gaze followed its path downward across his flat belly, it lingered helplessly on the maleness of his body. This intimacy was all so new to her and yet she felt no doubt, no confusion, no apprehension, only a growing, gathering need which had begun as a secret sweet ache between her thighs and was now swiftly spreading all through her body so that when Luke groaned and reached out to cup her breasts with his hands, her flesh was already receptive to his touch, her body quivering in silent expectation as he whispered against her skin. 'Melanie, don't look at me like that. I want to make this first time between us special. I want to make it last; I want to give you so much pleasure, but if you keep on looking at me in that way I won't be able to stop myself thinking about how it's going to feel, having your hands on my body—and not just your hands.' He groaned rawly, his teeth erotically savage as they tugged gently against her sensitive skin, his words conjuring up for her mental visions of such intimacy that her body grew hot and her eyes unconsciously mirrored the intensity of her thoughts.

Luke had stopped using his teeth on her vulnerable flesh and instead was sucking gently and slowly on one eagerly receptive nipple, while his free hand spread possessively against her lower stomach, and her body writhed in helpless sensual delight.

She wanted to touch him; to arouse him in the same way that he was arousing her.

'You've got the most wonderful skin,' Luke told her thickly. 'So sensitive, so responsive, I want to taste every last inch of it.'

She couldn't control the quiver that tormented her; already aroused by the sensual messages his touch was sending to her nervous system, her body jerked convulsively at his husky intimation that he desired and wanted to caress her so intimately.

As though her very silence was a secret verbal sign of assent he began slowly and tenderly to caress her whole body with his mouth, and although Melanie had no awareness of any impatience or urgency on his part, with every lingering caress of his tongue, with every subtle caress of his mouth, she found that he was feeding the need that was already burning so dangerously out of control within herself.

Many times more than once the sensation of his mouth against her skin made her twist frantically against him and cry out in urgent aching need for the completion for which her whole body hungered; but no matter how much she arched against him, her breath panting from her throat, her body taut with desire, he would not be hurried so that each caress, each lingering adoration threatened to drive her closer and closer to the edge of her self-control.

When his mouth eventually settled against the most intimate part of her body, she was so aroused and eager for his touch that she had no thought of stopping him, of protesting against such intimacy, his name a long drawn-out moan of pleasure wrenched from her throat as she gasped for air, torn between fighting the waves of pleasure shivering through her body and giving in to them—welcoming them, inviting them, she realised shudderingly as she heard the soft male sounds of satisfaction that Luke made against her flesh.

Quite when he stopped subjecting her to the sensual delight of that intimate caress and instead positioned her body so that he could show her how much their intimacy had aroused him, she had no idea.

All she knew was that, in some kind of hazy and completely natural way, it seemed only a heartbeat or so before the heat of his mouth was replaced by a different kind of heat, the urgency she had felt giving way to a sharper, keener urgency that made her move her body against his in an age-old rhythm and invitation.

It there was pain, she didn't feel it; all her senses were concentrated instead on savouring the immense, unexpected and totally overwhelming surges of pleasure his possession of her brought.

She felt her body convulse, her quickened breathing ceasing abruptly in a shocked gasp, and then Luke was calling to her, his body straining as though straining against some invisible bonds, his skin hot and damp where it touched her own, his flesh hard and urgent within the soft sheath of hers until suddenly he too reached the pinnacle she had just attained, bringing his body to a shuddering release.

When he drew her into his arms, holding her close, whispering soft words of praise in her ear, stroking his fingers through the silkiness of her hair, kissing the vulnerable curve of her throat and jaw, she lay trembling against him, too awed by all that had happened to speak, too shy all of a sudden to tell him, as he was telling her, how much pleasure he had given her.

She had no awareness of falling asleep, of being drawn even closer to Luke's body so that they lay together in the intimate tangle that belonged only to lovers, but when ultimately she did wake up it was to find that Luke was still there with her, holding her so securely that, for the first time in her whole life, the loneliness which had always been such an unwanted part of her, such a heavy burden to her, had been banished completely.

When he saw that she was awake, Luke smoothed the hair back off her face and whispered against her mouth, 'I didn't hurt you, did I?'

Melanie thought he must be referring to her cut leg, and shook her head, blushing a little as she recalled how quickly and easily she had forgotten her pain once Luke started to make love to her.

'No?' he pressed, feathering the words against her lips. 'Are you sure?'

His concern for her, his tenderness towards her, thrilled and delighted her. A huge bubble of happiness seemed to expand inside her, making her feel that if he let go of her she would probably float ecstatically up to the ceiling. But he wasn't letting go of her; he was holding on to her very firmly indeed, repeating huskily, 'Are you sure?'

'Sure, I'm sure,' Melanie teased him, laughing up at him as she asked innocently, 'What would you like me to do to prove it?'

Her breath caught abruptly in her throat, her skin turning fiery red as she saw the look in his eyes, and knew immediately that he wanted to make love to her again.

She couldn't quite conceal her shock from him, her lips parting, her mouth silently forming the word 'again' as she focused uncertainly on him.

'Only if you want to,' he assured her.

Only if she wanted to. A sudden and totally unexpected little tremor went through her body, telling her something about her own sensuality which she hadn't previously known. She caught her breath and

gazed at him with wide, slightly shocked eyes, but
when he caught hold of her hands and guided them
slowly to his body, showing her how much he
wanted her to caress him she found that just the
sensation of his skin beneath her fingertips was
enough to turn her own body to liquid heat and to
re-ignite the fires she had thought thoroughly sa-
tiated by their earlier lovemaking.

This time he was the one who moaned in eager
pleasure as she touched him first with her hands
and then later, when she grew more confident and
more aroused, with her mouth, until he trembled
openly, whispering to her that she was tormenting
him with what she was doing, telling her how much
he needed to hold her, to touch her, to make love
with her.

It was late in the afternoon when she woke up
again. Luke wasn't in bed with her this time. Instead he was sitting on the side of the bed, fully
dressed, watching her with an oddly sombre look
that made her heart skip a beat, and apprehension
took the place of the drowsy satiation with which
she had awoken.

'Luke, is something wrong?' she asked him
huskily. 'Is——?'

'No, nothing's wrong. There's just something I
have to do.' He stood up. 'I'm going to leave you
for a while, but when I come back . . . when I come
back we'll talk.'

Talk about what? she wondered worriedly once
he had gone. But, much as she longed to ask that
question, Melanie kept silent. Not once when he
had made love to her had Luke actually mentioned
the word 'love'. At the time it hadn't bothered her
because she had felt secure in his lovemaking, so

sure that she was loved that the words hadn't seemed necessary; but now, faced with his obvious withdrawal from her, with the apprehension which was quickly filling her, after he'd taken his leave of her, she couldn't help wondering anxiously if she had perhaps misjudged the situation; if perhaps he didn't love her after all; if... if what? What was the point in torturing herself like this? He was coming back and when he did they would talk. In the meantime...

In the meantime she was going to get up, have a bath, get dressed and have something to eat. And when Luke did come back...

Her whole body flushed as she realised just where her thoughts were taking her, just how receptive and eager she already was to the thought of further lovemaking. Would Luke suggest staying the night with her? Would he?

Quickly she got out of bed, ignoring the dull ache in her cut leg, and grimacing a little at the wide bandage Luke had tied round it. She was hardly likely to cut a glamorous and seductive figure with that, she thought, although fortunately it would be covered by her skirt. She wondered how long Luke would be and if she would have enough time for all the things she needed to do—such as washing her hair... changing the bed... She blushed again, still a little shocked by the sensuality of her own thoughts, and then limped a little awkwardly into the bathroom, pausing only to collect some fresh underwear on her way.

CHAPTER EIGHT

Two hours later Melanie's hair shone silkily, her make-up discreetly enhanced the glow of her skin and the brightness of her eyes, the soft full-skirted dress she was wearing was cinched in with a belt that emphasised the narrowness of her waist, and her skin was subtly perfumed with the scent of the expensive soap which had been a Christmas present from Louise.

In the sitting-room a fire burned cosily in the hearth. She had made herself a meal and eaten it. She had even changed the bed, though hurriedly averting her eyes from the small bright stain on the sheet she had been removing.

The sight of that stain had been rather unexpected. Somehow she had not expected her virginity to leave behind such a visible proof of its existence. It made the memory of their lovemaking even more intimate and erotic somehow... made her body quicken and her pulses race... made her shockingly aware of how easily Luke had awakened her to the intensity of her own sexuality.

She trembled in acknowledgement of how much she loved him, of how vulnerable that loving made her.

Another ten minutes passed, and then her stomach muscles jerked nervously as she heard the sound of a car draw up outside.

Somehow she managed not to give in to the temptation to rush to the window, but waited instead until she'd heard the brief knock on the front door.

It surprised her a little that Luke should use the front door, since in the past he had always come to the back, but she went to open it nonetheless, hoping that her eagerness, her mixed feelings of apprehension and delight didn't show too obviously in her face; yet when she opened the door it wasn't Luke who was standing there. It was a young woman. The same young woman she had seen staring so sneeringly at her from the passenger seat of a large BMW car.

'So you're still here, then,' the young woman said disparagingly as she pushed past Melanie and into the hallway. 'I suppose I shouldn't be too surprised. Luke said you were as hard as they come.'

Luke? Luke knew this woman... A cold feeling of dread seized Melanie as she turned to face her adversary. 'Look, I don't know who you are, or what you want——' she began uncomfortably.

'Liar! You know who I am well enough. I'm David Hewitson's daughter Lucinda, and Luke's fiancée; and as to what I want... What I want, Miss Foden is for Luke to get what's rightfully his.'

She heard Melanie's shocked gasp and said maliciously, 'What's wrong? Hasn't Luke told you yet about our engagement?' She waved her left hand in front of Melanie's stunned gaze. A huge sapphire and diamond ring sparkled on her third finger, the stones as cold as ice, the same ice which was slowly starting to encase Melanie's own heart, chilling her whole body, making her shiver with a mixture of shock and despair.

Did this woman...this fiancée know that Luke had spent the whole afternoon with her, making love to her? Was that why she was here, to warn her against taking anything Luke said or did too seriously, to warn her that he was practically a married man?

Suddenly Melanie had an urgent need to be physically sick. She turned her back on the other woman, saying thickly, 'Excuse me, but——'

'No, I won't excuse you, damn you!' Lucinda Hewitson told her viciously, digging long sharp nails into Melanie's arm as she caught hold of her and bodily imprisoned her.

She was a much taller girl than Melanie, bigger boned and heavier, but it wasn't physical fear that made Melanie wince and try to break free of her; it was the malice, the sheer hatred she could see glittering in the other woman's eyes. And yet didn't she have every right to hate her? Melanie acknowledged dully. After all, *she* was Luke's fiancée... Luke's fiancée... She had to swallow sharply on the bile souring her throat.

Was *that* what Luke had meant when he said he wanted to talk to her? Had he been going to tell her that he was engaged to someone else, to excuse his behaviour with her as mere male sexual desire, to beg her to keep what had happened a secret between them? Her desire to be sick increased. She was shivering, beset by a nausea and self-contempt so intense that it overwhelmed every single one of the other emotions she was feeling, including her need to keep her feelings, her thoughts private from this hard-eyed, vindictive woman.

'He doesn't give a damn about you really, you know,' Lucinda was telling her savagely. 'He laughs about you, actually. He says he can't believe how easy it's been to deceive you. He thought it was going to be far harder, but then, I suppose you just couldn't believe your luck, could you? And so you weren't on your guard against it. After all the time you must have spent in the old man's bed persuading him to leave you this place, I'll bet you couldn't believe your luck when Luke walked into your life, and you never even questioned it, did you? Never doubted for a moment what he told you.'

She was laughing now, a cynical hateful laugh that jarred on Melanie's sensitive ears, making her long to be able to cover them, to hide herself away somewhere where she could no longer hear the acid taunt of the other woman's voice.

'Luke was livid when he found out what you'd done, you know. Everyone knew he was the old man's only relative, that, even though they'd quarrelled and John Burrows had refused to speak to him, Luke believed he would never leave this place to someone outside the family.

'When Luke found out that you'd inherited it instead of him, he swore he'd get the will overset. He knew, you see, that his Uncle John would never have left this place to you had he been right in the head—"of sound mind" the legal people call it, don't they? Well, no old man of seventy-odd who thinks that a cheap scheming tart actually could ever really want him, no matter how much she lets him use her body, *could* be right in the head, could he?' she challenged viciously, while Melanie stared at her, her body frozen with shock, her mind turning instinctively away from the venomous things she was being told.

'You never even guessed, did you?' Lucinda was crowing triumphantly. 'It never occurred to you that Luke was lying to you...that he was here for one purpose and one purpose only, and that was to unmask you, to prove in court that the old man was out of his mind when he made that will.

'You can refuse to sell this place to my father as often as you like. In the end he'll get it, because in the end Luke will be able to establish the truth and get the old man's will overset, and then he'll sell out to Dad.

'Dad's promised us a brand new house in its own secluded piece of land on the other side of the village. He's giving it to us as a wedding present,' she added smugly.

'My God, when Luke told me how he'd come here and got you to swallow that story about him being a private detective and not having a telephone...! You really fell for it, didn't you? Well, I hope for your sake you haven't fallen for Luke as well, because he's mine, and all he wanted you for was to prove just what kind of woman you are...the kind who'd sleep with anyone—even an old man like John Burrows—if she thought there was anything in it for her. I knew the type you were when I saw you kissing that guy outside here the other day. Of course I told Luke immediately. Pity I didn't think to take a photograph...but then I expect by now Luke's got all the evidence he needs to prove in court the kind of pressure you put on the old man to get him to change his will.'

Melanie couldn't bear to listen to any more. If she didn't get rid of her tormentor right now she was going to be physically sick at her feet. Her brain was a sickening kaleidoscope of taunts and threats, her body reeling as though from a thousand physical blows.

Luke had lied to her. Luke had deceived her. Luke had made *love* to her purely and simply... She gagged on the acid burn of nausea clogging her throat and managed to demand thickly, 'Get out of here! Just get out... before I call the police and have you thrown out.'

'*You* call the police?' Lucinda taunted, but her voice had suddenly become nervously shrill and Melanie was pleased to see that she had released her arm and that she was starting to back away from her.

No doubt she did present a frightening picture if her face had gone as pale as it felt, if the emotions she could feel churning inside her body were even vaguely reflected in her eyes.

'Don't worry, I don't intend to stay,' Lucinda told her sneeringly. 'Luke will be here soon enough himself.'

'Luke!' Melanie gasped. She had forgotten all about Luke's return in the shock of Lucinda's arrival and what she had had to say. 'Just get out,' she repeated sickly.

To her relief Lucinda appeared to be doing just that. She opened the door and turned to Melanie, a cruel smile of triumph glittering in her eyes.

'Oh, yes, it's given Luke and me a few good laughs when he's told me how easily he deceived you.'

As she walked away from her, Melanie bit down hard on her lip to suppress her own choked response. It was no use telling herself that she should feel sorry for the other woman; that there was no way she could ever accept, never mind rejoice in the fact that a man she loved had so cruelly and callously deceived another human being, and there was certainly no way she could ever accept the fact that the man she loved had physically been intimate with another woman, no matter what the cause or the excuse. If she had known . . . if she had suspected for one moment that Luke was committed elsewhere . . .

She closed the door after her unwanted visitor, but before she could lock it she had to rush upstairs to the bathroom where she was violently sick.

After it was over and her heaving stomach had quietened a little, she washed her face and cleaned her teeth. She felt dizzy, her cut leg was throbbing painfully and she was starting to shiver again, not this time with cold but with shock.

How could Luke have done that to her? How could any man, no matter what the provocation? If he felt so strongly about his second cousin's will why couldn't he simply have told her . . . asked her? She would soon have been able to tell him the truth that she had no more idea than he had as to why she should have been chosen to inherit. And as for Lucinda Hewitson's vile accusations—no, she corrected herself shakily, *Luke's* vile accusations about her supposed relationship with John Burrows . . .

She shuddered nauseously again. How could he have imagined . . . how could he have believed . . . how could he have brought himself to talk to her, never mind touch her . . . never mind make love to her in the way that he had, believing that she . . . ?

As she relived every one of Lucinda's cruel taunts she asked herself despairingly if Luke really thought his own behaviour was any better than that which

he had attributed to her, if he really thought his
motives were any purer, any less sickeningly vile,
or if he truly believed that each and every lie he
had uttered could honestly be vindicated. Wasn't
he just as motivated by greed as he had so wrongly
assumed her to be? Wasn't he even worse in his
way than the woman he thought her to be? John
Burrows had been his second cousin, and yet, even
though they had quarrelled and he had obviously
neglected the old man, he had still arrogantly
expected to be his heir.

Melanie thought of all the long bitter years during
which her benefactor had obviously been alone...of
the way he had clung to this family home, even
while he had stubbornly refused to make things up
with his only remaining family; and, as the hot tears
began to sting her throat and her eyes, she knew
that there was only one thing she could do.

She had to get away from this house, from its
memories, from the pain that just thinking about
it would now always bring her. Tomorrow...first
thing tomorrow she would drive into Knutsford and
put the house in the hands of an estate agent. She
wasn't going to wait for an auction to be arranged
nor for the new motorway route to be disclosed,
but one thing she was determined upon and that
was that no way, *no way* was she going to allow
either Luke or his fiancée and her greedy father to
benefit from such a sale. She would have a docu-
ment drawn up, legally preventing whoever bought
the house from selling it for at least five years. She
would...

Frantically she drove her brain into a flurry of
thoughts and decisions, frantically, despairingly
trying to hold at bay the avalanche of anguish she

knew was waiting to descend on her, to bury her, to flood her with pain like no pain she had ever known before.

She remembered how Luke had held her only hours ago, how he had touched her, caressed her, spoken to her. She remembered how she had told herself that even if he had not spoken the word 'love' it had been there between them, almost a tangible presence; and then she started to shudder as paroxysm after paroxysm of sick self-disgust seized her.

How *could* she have been so stupid, so naïve, so trusting? A private detective…and yet he had never once mentioned any case to her, and she, fool that she was, had believed him…had believed him when he'd claimed to be as much a stranger to the area as she was herself. *Now* she understood the reason for all those probing questions about her background, her family. *Now* she understood why he had kept on returning. Now she understood those times when he had seemed to stand aloof and withdrawn from her, when he had looked at her with cold angry eyes, when she had felt almost that he was two different and separate people. What a complete fool she had been. But no more: Lucinda had opened her eyes to the truth, thankfully before it was too late—for the cottage at least. As far as her own feelings were concerned…

Gulping back a sob, she walked painfully into the sitting-room. The fire still burned as cheerfully, the room still looked as cosily welcoming as it had done before Lucinda's arrival, but there was no way that Melanie could sit down in it now, knowing that she had prepared it with so much love and joy for Luke's arrival, for Luke's presence, just as she had prepared herself for Luke's pleasure, she thought bitterly, unable to contain the destructive emotions rioting inside her.

And as for her bedroom... She gagged sickly on the nausea still burning inside her, knowing that there was no way she could sleep in that room tonight, nor ever again. She would rather sleep outside on the cold wet earth than sleep in that room, in that bed.

She clutched her stomach as her grief burned through her like a physical pain, her body bent almost double, the firelight shining on the smooth fall of her hair and revealing the pale curve of her cheek and the almost bloodless agony of her mouth, and that was how Luke saw her five minutes later when he pushed open the sitting-room door and walked in.

He had knocked on the back door and, receiving no response, had opened it and walked in; and now, seeing Melanie in obvious distress and pain, he rushed up to her, exclaiming anxiously, 'Melanie... My God! What's wrong? Your leg...!'

CHAPTER NINE

FOR a moment shock seized Melanie, completely paralysing her, but then, as Luke stepped forward and touched her, a bolt of fierce rejection ran through her, freeing her, so that she could step back from him and say in a choked voice. 'Don't touch me... Don't come anywhere near me!'

Frantic with self-contempt and misery, she hugged her arms protectively around her body at the same time as she wrenched herself away from him.

'Melanie, for God's sake—what's wrong?'

Oh, but he was a good actor! No one looking at him now could possibly doubt his concern, his confusion. No one, that was, other than someone like herself, or Lucinda, who knew the truth.

'What's wrong?' She laughed hysterically. 'You can ask me that? I should have thought there was a good deal wrong when a woman allows herself to be used by a man like you...a man who, moreover, obviously considers himself to have some sort of right to sit in moral judgement on others...a man who seems to believe he has some right to take the law into his own hands to interpret and abuse as he sees fit...a man who can quite callously ignore the loneliness and unhappiness of someone, can then ignore that person for years on end and can also claim to know them so well that he has the right to interfere in their most private and personal affairs...a man who can actually be physically in-

timate with a woman he claims to despise and
detest . . . and you are that kind of man, aren't you,
Luke? When that kind of man can lie and cheat,
can do anything he chooses to do, then, yes, I
should say there is most certainly something
wrong . . . with him,' she finished shakily. 'I should
say there is a good deal wrong with him, wouldn't
you, Luke? Oh, and by the way, for your information I did *not* seduce your second cousin into
leaving me this place. I did not even know him, and
if you don't believe me then I suggest you check
with his solicitors. In fact, I suggest you would have
been far better employed checking with them in the
first place, or even simply asking me.

'But then of course you never really wanted the
truth, did you, Luke? What you wanted was to find
some excuse for having Mr Burrows's will overset
so that you could inherit in my place, so that you
could ensure that your prospective father-in-law
could get exactly what he wanted.

'I should have known, I suppose.' She was
shaking violently now, her teeth chattering together
as she forced each word out. Her leg ached as
though it were being savaged by sharp teeth, her
head ached, her throat was sore, but none of that
was anything compared to the pain burning her
heart, searing her with the acid of self-contempt.

'I don't understand. What the hell are you trying
to say to me?' Luke interrupted her brusquely.
'When I left here this afternoon——'

'When you left here this afternoon your fiancée
had not been to see me,' Melanie told him bitterly.
'But now that she has, it's no use lying any more,
Luke. I know it all . . . every last mean and sordid
detail.'

When she looked at him, Melanie saw that his face had gone a shocked shade of grey-white.

'My *what*?' he demanded.

'Your fiancée,' Melanie repeated in a voice as brittle as old glass. 'Miss Lucinda Hewitson. She even showed me her engagement ring, and she told me about the house her father plans to give you.'

'Personally, knowing what I do now know about you, I'd run a hundred miles from marriage to a man capable of behaving the way you've behaved, Luke, but then obviously the pair of you share a very special moral code; one that isn't easily understood by people like me.'

She had to turn away from him then in case the anguish that was destroying her inside became visible in her eyes. All she had left now was her pride; a pride that was demanding a very heavy price from her for supporting her now, as she struggled to put aside the deep love she felt towards Luke and to concentrate instead on the reality of the man Lucinda Hewitson had revealed to her, a man so flawed, so devoid of every virtue which Melanie held sacrosanct that she still could not comprehend how she had come to be so easily deceived by him.

'I want you to leave now, Luke. After all, there is no point in your staying. And as for your scheme to get Mr Burrows's will overset...' She turned back to him, her shoulders straight and her spine tense, pride only just masking the intensity of the pain he had caused her as she told him tiredly. 'You see, you were wrong about me, Luke, and about my relationship with your second cousin. I never knew John Burrows. Never met him. Never even knew he existed until after his death, and if you had come to me honestly and openly in the the first place, instead of playing amateur detective, instead of lying and cheating your way into my life——' Into my heart, she could have said, but she just managed to resist. If she had been foolish enough to fall in love with him, then that was as much her fault as it was his. 'If you had come to me openly in the first place,' she repeated firmly, 'then I would have told you the truth.'

She started to turn away from him again, too drained to go on, and then froze as unbelievably Luke reached out and took hold of her shoulders, ignoring the freezing rejection of her body and her eyes as he forced her to turn round to face him.

'Melanie, you've got to listen to me. You don't understand,' he began, but she stopped him, her face set and her voice crystal clear with revulsion as she told him icily,

'Oh, yes I do. I understand that you've deliberately lied to me...deceived me...used me. I understand that you're John Burrows's second cousin, that you expected to inherit this cottage and the land, that you planned to sell it to David Hewitson so that between you you'd make a rich killing when the new motorway extension is approved. You came here intending to discredit me, to have Mr. Burrows's will overset. Well, it won't work. You disgust me, do you know that?' she told him shakily. 'And if I've one regret in my life it's that I was gullible enough, vulnerable enough to believe in your lies. Well, I promise you this, I'll never be that credulous again. There were no lengths you weren't prepared to go to to get what you wanted, were there, Luke? None at all. Even to the extent of having sex with me—presumably so that

you could stand up in court and tell everyone just
what kind of woman I am...the kind of woman
who wouldn't hesitate to——' Abruptly she stopped.
Not even the intensity of her pain and anger could
allow her to put into words the full horror of what
was in her mind, that Luke had made love to
her...no, had had sex with her—despite what she
had felt at the time, there had been nothing loving,
nothing tender, nothing caring about the intimacy
they had shared—as a means of helping to prove
that she *was* the kind of woman who would deliberately set out to sexually seduce a vulnerable old
man out of material greed.

'Since she seems to know exactly what's been
going on, I can only wonder that Lucinda Hewitson
should still want to marry you, but, as I've already
said, you're quite obviously a well-matched pair;
made for one another, in fact,' she told him
scornfully.

'Melanie, you've got things all wrong!'

She couldn't believe it; *couldn't* believe that he
would actually have the gall to go on trying to deceive her when his own fiancée had told her the
truth.

'Have I?' she demanded wearily. 'Very well, then,
Luke. Tell me that you aren't John Burrows's
second cousin.'

There was a brief silence, and then he spoke
huskily.

'I can't.'

'No,' Melanie agreed softly, her mouth curling
into a bitter little smile. 'You can't, can you, Luke?'

'Melanie, my relationship with John is a fact. I
can't deny that, but as for the rest——'

'You're wasting your time, Luke,' she told him dully. 'I really don't want to hear any more.'

'Did what happened between us today mean so little to you that you won't even give me a chance to explain?'

Her throat ached as she drew in a sharp breath. Even now he still wanted to torment her. She looked at him, unable to hide the pain and the disillusionment in her eyes. 'As far as I'm concerned, today is a day I intend to wipe completely from my memory. I never want to see or hear from you again, Luke. Oh, and by the way, I intend to make very, very sure that you never get your hands on the cottage. Your second cousin must have had a good reason for not leaving it to you, for choosing to leave it to a complete stranger, someone whose name he could only have picked out at random from some telephone directory, I suspect. Doesn't it tell you anything, Luke, that he would rather leave his home, a home he obviously cherished and loved, to a stranger, than to his only living relative?

'Poor man. No children of his own, only a second cousin, who apparently cared so little for him that he left him to live out the last years of his life unhappy and alone.'

She heard Luke give an exasperated sigh.

'Melanie, it wasn't like that,' he told her roughly. 'If John was alone it was because he chose to be. He damn near quarrelled with everyone he knew. Why, he even——' He broke off suddenly and frowned. He was looking directly at her, but Melanie had the distinct impression that he was not really seeing her at all. No doubt he was plotting some further underhand way to get the cottage off her. Well, with a bit of luck, soon it would be sold to someone else, and she would be free to leave here, to go away and get on with her own life.

'I want you to leave, Luke. Now. Or do I have to repeat the threat I had to make to your fiancée to call the police?'

'What?' He focused on her for a second. 'Yes, all right, I'll go, but this isn't the end of things. When you've had time to calm down and reflect . . . I can't deny that I did deceive you, but not in the way you seem to think.'

He had made no effort to move towards the door, and in fact looked as though he was not about to move at all.

'And as for Lucinda Hewitson being my fiancée . . .' He paused, while Melanie looked at him with shocked eyes.

'But she told me——'

'I don't care what she told you. She and I are not engaged, never have been engaged and never will be engaged,' he told her flatly. 'Neither do I have any kind of involvement with her father, nor . . .'

'Don't say any more, Luke,' Melanie advised him shakily when he paused for breath. 'I really don't think I want to hear any more lies from you.'

'I haven't told you any lies,' he told her bluntly. 'Oh, yes, there may have been certain omissions of various facts, but——'

'You told me you were a private detective up here to work on a case,' Melanie interrupted him with a passionate bitterness. 'Was that the truth?'

The scorn in her voice brought an angry surge of colour up under his skin.

'No, not entirely,' he admitted curtly. 'It's true that I'm not a private detective. In fact, my partner and I run a company which provides advanced security of a variety of types for those who need it. And as for the case on which I was working...'

He paused and looked at her.

Enlightenment came slowly, but once it had come, Melanie stared at him, anger and indignation colouring her too-pale face.

'You mean, you were investigating me?' she demanded. 'I don't want to hear any more, Luke! I——'

'Maybe you don't but you're going to,' he told her dangerously, taking hold of her before she could stop him, and virtually propelling her back towards the fireplace.

Melanie couldn't stop him; she had neither the physical nor the emotional resources with which to do so. Physically he could overpower her any time he chose, and if his grip on her was firmly determined, rather than in any way threatening or intimidating, it was still enough to make her wary.

And as for physically trying to push him away, the mere thought of actually having to touch him was sufficient to bring back her earlier churning nausea. Luke must have read what she was feeling in her eyes, because, as he pushed her down into one of the armchairs, she said cynically. 'What's wrong? Can't bring yourself to soil your hands by touching me, is that it? My God, you don't believe in giving anyone much of a chance to defend themselves, do you?'

'What defence could you possibly have?' Melanie had intended the words to sound cold and hard, but instead her voice had a dangerous wobble to it, almost a hidden plea to him that he would actually explain away the whole unbelievably hurtful affair. But logic told her that this was impossible.

'Yes, it's true that it did originally cross my mind, when I heard that a very young and pretty woman had inherited Uncle John's assets, that this same young woman might well be scheming and manipulative; and yes, I did decide to carry out some investigations of my own into exactly why he should have made her his heiress; and yes, I freely admit that I did, in a much regretted moment of weakness, say as much to Lucinda Hewitson, but not because there was or ever has been any intimacy between us. Lucinda isn't my type—she's a selfish, spoiled, amoral parasite who leaves me completely cold, both emotionally and physically,' he said bluntly. 'No, the sole reason I ever mentioned the matter to Lucinda was that she was trying to enveigle me into trying to persuade you to sell up to her father. If she got the idea that had I inherited from John I would have sold out to Hewitsons, then she certainly did not get it from me. As it happens, I suspect that the land wouldn't be of much use to them anyway, since I've heard a whisper that the Committee intends to opt for the second choice of route for the motorway extension, but that isn't common knowledge as yet.

'As for the rest, I admit that my initial assessment of the situation was totally wrong and totally unforgivable, and, if I'm honest with you, I think it was prompted more by my own guilt than anything else.

'Of course, once I'd met you... Well, let's just say my emotions had a very hard time accepting what my brain was trying to tell them. None of the facts seemed to add up. I couldn't reconcile the kind

of woman I was discovering you to be with the
shrewd little gold-digger of my imagination, and
the more I got to know you the harder it became
to retain that image.

'But then of course there was my own guilt and
its demand that I at least made some attempt to
find out why John had made you his heiress—not
because I resented what he had done; I didn't. But
you were right about one thing: I *had* neglected him.
I *had* let pride, if you like, come between us.

'After my father died, John was very good to
me. My mother and I lived quite near to here until
she remarried. I suppose in many ways John became
my substitute father, just as I ...' He paused and
then continued heavily. 'It was when I made my
decision to leave the army that we first quarrelled.
There had always been a tradition in the Burrows
family that the men went into that service. John
himself fought during the Second World War, and
was later invalided out of the army. He grew up
here, of course.

'When I refused to change my mind about leaving
the army, he told me he never wanted to see me
again. He was prone to be very quick-tempered,
very unforgiving and intolerant of the views of
others. I tried to make him understand, but he just
wouldn't listen to me, and so I did as he had demanded and left him strictly alone. I was younger
then and probably far too stubborn myself.

'It was my mother who pointed out to me how
lonely he was and how much he was probably
missing me, even though nothing would ever make
him admit it.

'I came down to see him several times; my
business was based in London then and, like all

new businesses, demanded a very large slice of my time. He always let me in, but once I was in he would sit in that chair you're sitting in and simply not say a word. You see, he had told me that he wouldn't speak to me again unless I went back into the army, and since I couldn't do that . . .

'While my mother was still living locally there was a point of contact between us, but once she left . . . Perhaps I should have tried harder to make him understand, but he could be unbelievably stubborn, unbelievably unforgiving. When he died—well, he was a good age, of course, but I just hadn't expected it. It came as such a shock; made me realise that suddenly he wasn't going to be there any more. I suppose I'd always had the idea at the back of my mind, that somehow or other I'd get him to accept that the army just was not for me, that we'd make up our differences. To realise that that just wasn't going to happen was hard, very hard, but what was even harder to accept was the loneliness of the last years of his life; a loneliness I could have, should have done something about.

'It was my guilt, because I *hadn't* done that, that made me want to know more about you, Melanie; not any resentment because he'd left everything to you. I suppose in a way I was hoping that there would be some valid connection between you, not so that I could overset the will as you seem to think—that had never even crossed my mind——'

'But Lucinda said——' Melanie began, but Luke cut her short, telling her harshly,

'I don't give a damn what Lucinda told you. She was lying. Condemn me if you must, but at least condemn me for the sins I have committed, and not those I haven't. Greed was never my motivation.'

He gave her a tight smile. 'In fact, it might surprise you to learn that these days I'm a rather wealthy man in my own right. Our business venture has proved unexpectedly successful.'

'But you obviously thought that greed had motivated me,' Melanie pointed out tightly.

Luke looked at her consideringly and then asked gently, 'Not greed necessarily. Once I knew about your background, once I understood how hard and deprived your childhood was, I could understand why you might feel a need to be cautiously careful with money. I knew for instance that you must have inherited some money from John, and yet when I suggested buying a new carpet for the bedroom you immediately balked as though you could not afford one.'

Melanie went white with anguish. 'Because I don't consider that money mine to spend,' she told him fiercely. 'Just as I *don't* consider this cottage mine——' She broke off, flushing darkly as she realised how much she had betrayed.

Luke was frowning at her.

'What on earth do you mean? Of course they're yours. John left them to you.'

Melanie shook her head.

'Not, not to me,' she told him. 'Not to me the individual, the person; he left them to a stranger, any stranger; a stranger picked at random for no reason other than that he must have just chanced across my name somehow or other.' Tears filled her eyes as she continued huskily, 'At first I kept on thinking that there'd been some mistake; that his solicitors must have confused me with another Melanie Foden, that he could not possibly have intended to leave everything—this cottage, his money—to a stranger, and then when I discovered how alone he had been it was as though I had found a link which tied us together, and I knew then what I had to do.

'I intend to sell the cottage. Oh, not to someone like David Hewitson, but to someone who will care for it and turn it into a proper home, and the money that I get for it, plus the money your cousin left me, I intend to donate to a charity in his name.' She stopped abruptly. Why was she telling him all this? It was almost as though secretly she wanted to vindicate herself to him. Why should she want that when he was the one in the wrong, the one who had cruelly and deliberately deceived her?

'Just as soon as I find a suitable buyer for the cottage I intend to sell it and leave here,' she told him flatly.

'I don't think your cousin did me any favours in naming me as his sole beneficiary.' She gave a bitter laugh. 'If he hadn't done so, at least I'd have been spared the discovery that the man I——' She stopped again, biting her lip angrily as she realised how close she had just come to admitting her love for him, and amended her sentence to carry on unevenly, 'The discovery of just how much you've lied to me, and exactly what you think of me. You know, you really have surprised me, Luke. Thinking what you think about me in this day and age, when none of us can escape from knowing the consequences of having sex with partners with a history of previous lovers, I shouldn't have thought you'd want to take the risk involved in being intimate with a woman whom you believed went around seducing old men in order to inherit their money——'

'Oh, for God's sake!' Luke interrupted her brusquely. 'I *never* thought any such thing. Not once I'd met you, talked to you; and even if I had,' he added quietly, 'I'm hardly likely to go on thinking so, am I? Unless of course you've perfected a from of seduction that somehow or other leaves your virginity intact.'

Melanie half rose from her chair and then froze.

'This afternoon,' Luke continued softly, 'what we shared together was so special to me that I had hoped, believed——'

'I don't want to talk about it,' Melanie told him abruptly. The truth was that she *dared* not let him talk about it. She was terrified that if she did she would weaken completely, and she could not afford to do that . . . she could not afford to allow herself to be vulnerable to him again. He had deceived her once; she shuddered as she remembered how much, and even though his explanation had been logical, acceptable in many ways, she was still being driven by her emotions, emotions which told her bitterly that she had accepted him, loved him without question or doubt, whereas he . . .

She drew a deep shaky breath.

'Melanie, I think you know what I'm trying to say to you. All right, so maybe what happened this afternoon was a trifle precipitate, a case, perhaps, of putting the cart before the horse, but when I saw you falling on to that piece of glass . . .' He stopped speaking, a muscle working in his throat, his eyes shadowed with pain.

'That degree of shock has a way of undermining a man's self-control, and from the moment I met you mine has been subjected to some pretty tough harassment.'

'If you're trying to tell me that you wanted to have sex with me——' Melanie began bravely, but he cut right through her challenging sentence and told her furiously,

'No, I am damn well not trying to tell you that I "wanted to have sex" with you. What I wanted was to make love with you and, although I have the feeling that right now you'd rather walk to hell and back barefoot than admit it, I got the impression that you wanted it as well. I'm not the kind of man who thinks of sex as a physical appetite to be appeased. That way of living has never had any appeal for me.

'What I am trying to say is that I love you, and that I'd hoped you were coming to love me too. OK, I haven't been as honest with you as perhaps I should, but, whether you choose to believe it or not, I was coming back here tonight to tell you everything. God knows why Lucinda Hewitson took it upon herself to come round here and give you that cock and bull story about our being engaged. As I told her father when I went to see him earlier, I completely support you in your decision not to sell out to him——' He broke off, his face clearing. 'My God, I wonder if that's it?' He gave her a direct look. 'In normal circumstances this wouldn't be something I'd ever think worth mentioning, but Lucinda, being the type of woman she is, is rather prone to making her desires plain and unfortunately some time ago she did let it be known that she wouldn't be averse to a relationship developing between the two of us. Of course, I told her as tactfully as I could that it just wasn't on. I wonder if this is her way of paying me back? She was there today when I saw her father and I made it pretty plain to them both, I suspect, just how I feel about you.'

'She was wearing an engagement ring,' Melanie told him shakily.

'Mm. This engagement ring—it wouldn't have been a particularly vulgar and unattractive sapphire surrounded by diamonds, would it?'

When Melanie nodded, he grinned.

'A birthday present from her doting father, or so she told me when she was showing it off to *me* this afternoon. Only then she was wearing it on her right hand.'

It was Melanie's turn to frown as she remembered that she had noticed that the ring was a little loose on the other woman's finger.

He loved her, Luke had said. Loved her. But how could she believe him, and, even if she believed him, how could she trust him? How could she be sure that he would go on loving her? She couldn't, and it was too much of a risk to take, too great a step into the unknown.

She looked up and froze. Luke was coming towards her. If he touched her now, held her, kissed her... She was shaking inside at the intensity of her own vulnerability, her own need. She stood up, warding him off instinctively, telling him shakily, 'Don't touch me, Luke—not now. I don't think I could bear it.'

In any other circumstances, the look in his eyes could have made her weep. As it was she shuddered visibly, tensing under the strain of holding on to her self-control and her pride, of not allowing herself to fall into his arms and tell him that she loved him and that nothing else mattered. But once she did that, once she allowed her heart to rule her head ... He had lied to her once, even if it was only by omission. She had never dreamed, never guessed that he was John Burrows's second cousin, never contemplated that he might be deliberately cultivating her friendship for any other reason than that he was attracted to her, and that knowledge hurt her unbearably. She had been so naïve, so trusting, while Luke ...

'I know you need time,' she heard Luke saying. 'I think I can understand a little of what you're going through, but, believe me, Melanie, my need to find out what kind of woman you are and why John had named you as his beneficiary never had a thing to do with any desire to have his will overset. It was prompted only by my guilt ... never by greed.'

'You could have told me the truth. You should have told me the truth,' Melanie told him tonelessly.

'I wanted to, but the longer I waited the harder it became. Equally,' he gave her a twisted smile, 'equally you could have told me the truth—or at least you could have told me why you didn't want to touch John's money. But you obviously didn't feel that you could; didn't trust me enough. We both kept certain truths hidden from one another, didn't we?'

It was an accusation she couldn't refute.

'There is something else,' Luke continued. 'Something my mother reminded me about. I wanted to discuss it with you but——'

'Whatever it is, I don't want to hear about it,' Melanie cut in wearily.

She didn't think she could stand any more explanations right now. She was finding it increasingly hard to preserve an outward show of calm, to stop herself from breaking down in front of him.

'Please go, Luke.' Her voice was flat, devoid of all emotion, but her eyes betrayed the truth to him. He took a step towards her and then, as she shrank back from him, he stopped, his mouth hardening with compression.

'All right, Melanie,' he told her. 'I'll go, but I promise you this: I'll be back, and when I do come back I intend to make you understand that, no matter what has gone wrong between us, you and I have a future together... a good future. I'm not about to repeat with you the mistakes I made with John. I'm not going to let a quarrel, a grievance—no matter how justified—come between us. I love you, and that's something I've never said to any woman before. I love you and I want you in my life. Now and forever.'

After he had gone, Melanie wondered wearily why his last words to her had sounded more like a threat than a promise; why they rang, doom-laden, through her mind like a funereal bell.

She loved him. She couldn't deny that, but she could no more accept and encourage that love than she could actually have done as he had initially assumed—callously set out to deprive an old man of his wealth.

She didn't have the emotional stamina for a relationship in which she could not be sure of her partner's true feelings, of his true commitment to her; so, no matter how much she might love Luke, no matter how much he might claim he loved her, she dared not allow herself to believe that their love could possibly have a future.

Later, as she prepared for bed, she promised herself tiredly that first thing in the morning she was going to carry through her intention of putting the cottage up for sale. Only when she was free of its burden would she be able to physically escape from the emotional pressure she suspected Luke's continued presence would put upon her.

CHAPTER TEN

SO IT was done. The cottage was now in the hands of an estate agent, who had promised her that he expected to achieve a sale within a very reasonable period of time, even with the stipulations she had made as to the resale of the property.

Knutsford was busy with shoppers and traffic, but people were the last thing she wanted at the moment. Unexpectedly she discovered that what she craved was the solitude, the protective privacy of the cottage.

Rather than sleep in the bed she had shared with Luke, she had spent the night curled up in front of the sitting-room fire, wrapped in her duvet, as a result of which she now felt stiff all over and very tired.

When she had driven back to the cottage she parked her car and climbed out. She doubted if there'd been a second since his departure last night when she had stopped thinking about Luke. She had tried not to, tried to insist to herself that all she was doing was making it worse for herself, increasing her pain. Over and over again she could hear his voice telling her he loved her. The harder she struggled to hold on to the fact that he had deceived her, the louder those words seemed to become until now they were threatening to drown out the reality of the situation completely.

Just as she was about to head for the cottage, she heard a car coming down the lane.

Instinctively she hurried to the gate and opened it, stepping out into the lane to see who was approaching.

It wasn't Luke, not unless he had borrowed the large BMW belonging to David Hewitson, who once again was driving far too fast down what was after all only a very narrow lane. Where was he going? she wondered curiously, on the point of turning round to go back into the garden.

Later she was never quite sure what had happened; whether she had inadvertently stepped out into the lane; whether David Hewitson's sudden increase in speed, like his swerve in to her side of the road, had been deliberate or accidental. All she did know was that she had turned round to discover that the BMW seemed to be heading straight for her, and that, as fast as she had tried to move out of its way, she could not move quite fast enough.

She had felt the impact of the car's heavy metal frame against the side of her body, a sickening, jarring agony that had made her cry out in pain as the impact sent her headlong into the undergrowth which separated her garden from the lane.

She discovered later that it was two walkers who had discovered her inert body, and had gone for help, quite naturally, to the only other house they had passed, which just happened to be Luke's rented cottage.

It was Luke apparently who had summoned an ambulance and insisted on riding in it with her when they took her to hospital; Luke who had waited by her bedside until he'd been quite sure that she had suffered no permanent damage; Luke who had questioned the walkers but could not discover from them just what had happened to her, and it was also Luke who was still sitting at her bedside in the hospital when she eventually came round to find Luke's face haggard with shock and anxiety.

'Luke.'

The moment she said his name, he was reaching out towards her, lifting her hand off the bed and holding it tenderly between his own.

'What happened?' she asked him anxiously. 'What am I doing here?'

'That's what we'd all like to know,' he told her grimly. 'You were found unconscious at the roadside by a pair of walkers. How you got there...'

The fog was starting to clear from round her brain.

'It was David Hewitson,' she told him dully, shuddering as she explained what had happened.

'He ran you down deliberately?' Luke was frowning at her, but not sounding as disbelieving as she had expected.

'I ... I don't know. I'm not sure. He seemed ...' she licked her dry lips ' ... he seemed to increase his speed to head right for me. I tried to get out of the way, but I couldn't move fast enough. My leg...'

'This will have to be reported to the police,' Luke told her gravely. 'The man's a maniac.'

Immediately Melanie caught hold of his sleeve. 'No, Luke, please don't! I don't think I could stand all the fuss... I suppose he was angry with me because I wouldn't sell to him. I don't think he planned to hurt me, he just——'

'Saw his opportunity and took it. Melanie, he could have killed you!'

'But he didn't,' she told him tiredly. 'Please promise me you'll just let it go, Luke. After all, even I can't be sure that he did intend to hurt me.'

'*You* may not be,' Luke told her grimly. 'Others won't be so generous; certainly I shan't. The man's notorious for his temper.' He saw her face and said quietly, 'All right, if it's what you want. You've put the cottage up for sale, then?' he asked her, abruptly changing the subject.

Melanie nodded.

'Yes. Yes. I felt it was for the best.'

'Mm. They've told me that they don't think it's necessary to keep you in here overnight. They need the bed apparently,' he added drily. 'Once the doctor's been to check you over, they'll be sending you home—back to the cottage.'

Although she said nothing, Melanie felt like bursting into tears. Suddenly she was very afraid... very much aware of being alone. Right now the last thing she wanted was to go back to the solitude of the cottage but not because she was afraid that David Hewitson might try to harm her: she was thoroughly convinced that if he had tried deliberately to hurt her, it had been a momentary impulse, a burst of aggression and temper, not something which had been premeditated, for all the threats he had previously made against her.

Within half an hour, as Luke had predicted, the doctor had been round to check her over and, having pronounced her undamaged apart from some bruises, had told her that he was sending her home.

'Is there someone who could come and collect you——?' he started to enquire, but Luke did not allow him to finish, saying firmly,

'I'm taking her home,' and, before Melanie could object, he said quietly. 'I've got the car here anyway. Don't waste your breath arguing about it, Melanie.'

In truth, arguing with him was quite beyond her at the moment. As the doctor had warned her, she was still very much in a state of shock; a state in which it seemed far easier to let other people take control of her and her life, rather than to force herself into the kind of mental and physical effort she simply did not think she was capable of sustaining.

She didn't even object when, once they were outside the hospital, Luke insisted on picking her up and carrying her over to his car. Her sore leg was aching badly since she had apparently fallen heavily on it, causing it to start bleeding again.

Having ensured that she was fastened securely into the passenger seat, Luke walked round to the driver's side and got in beside her.

'Go to sleep if that's what you feel like doing,' he advised her, turning towards her to adjust the head-rest and the seat so that she could do just that.

Perhaps because of her state of shock, she didn't know, but, whatever the reason, she seemed intensely aware of him physically as he leaned over her. Not just of the strength and height of him, but of the scent of his body, the measure of his breathing, and if she closed her eyes she could even remember the shape and texture of his body beneath his clothes, the sensation of his flesh beneath her fingertips, the living, breathing warmth of him.

She shivered violently, causing him to stop what he was doing and touch her face in swift alarm.

'Melanie, are you OK?'

Bitter tears gathered in her throat. How could she tell him the truth: that the only way she would ever be 'OK' again would be if he took her in his arms and somehow made her forget everything that lay between them.

'I'm fine,' she lied, turning her face away from him and staring blindly out of the window.

She felt thoroughly disorientated by her accident. It seemed impossible to believe that it was still only early in the afternoon. She felt as though she had lived through several traumatic lifetimes in the last few days, all her mental and physical reserves so totally depleted that she simply had nothing left to fall back on.

Once they were back at the cottage, Luke refused to let her get out of the car unaided, carrying her, as he had done from the hospital, to the door, and from there upstairs and into the bedroom he had decorated for her, gently depositing her on the bed, before she could open her mouth to object.

And what, after all, could she say? she wondered bitterly. That she couldn't sleep in this bed because he had shared it with her? What a self-betrayal that would be.

'I'm going to have to leave you for a while,' he told her as he secured the duvet around her. 'But I'll be back just as soon as I can——'

'Back? But, Luke, there's no need for that.'

'No need! If you think for one moment I'm going to let you sleep here alone...'

Her heart was beating frantically fast.

'But you can't stay here,' she protested. 'There's nowhere for you to sleep. The other bed's broken, and Mr Burrows——'

'I'll sleep downstairs,' he told her flatly. 'I'm not leaving you on your own, Melanie.'

She was too weak to continue arguing with him. He insisted on making her a cup of tea, but she had fallen asleep before she could drink it, worn out with shock and pain.

When he came upstairs and found her fast asleep, Luke stared down at her for a long time, and then very gently touched her face with his fingertips.

In her sleep she sighed and turned towards his hand so that her lips were touching his skin. His body tensed as love and desire flooded through him. No matter how long it took, somehow he would find a way to convince her. To make her see that what they felt for one another was too precious, too important to be jeopardised by any kind of misunderstanding.

But right now he had things to do, enquiries to set in motion—a thought which had occurred to him the previous evening when he had listened to her sad little voice telling him how John must surely have picked her name at random.

That did not accord with the man he knew. John Burrows had never acted on impulse and certainly not on that kind of impulse. He was a man to whom family had been all important. Family. That was the key to this whole mystery, Luke was sure of it.

He had another matter to attend to as well, something which he hoped would go some way to proving to Melanie how much she meant to him. It was pointless cursing the fate now which had ever led him into making that idiotic and betraying comment to Lucinda Hewitson. He had sensed from the moment he met her that Melanie could never have been the type of woman to deceive and seduce a lonely old man. Had known it, but had fought against it, just as he had tried to fight against loving her until he had realised that what he was trying to deny himself was one of the greatest gifts that life could offer. But by then it had been too late; by then Lucinda had been at work, spreading her poison.

He sighed as he gently and tenderly kissed Melanie's half-parted lips. Somehow he would find a way to break through the barriers she was erecting against him. Somehow there must be a way. There had to be a way.

'I had a telephone call this morning. The estate agents have a buyer for the house. He's prepared to pay the full asking price, and to abide by the conditions I've laid down.'

'You still intend to sell, then?'

It was three days later, and this morning, for the first time since Melanie's accident, Luke had actually allowed her to get out of bed and come downstairs.

It was bright and sunny outside but with a cold wind, so Luke had insisted that she was to stay inside in front of the fire he had made up for her.

He had been out first thing and had returned with a pile of extravagant and expensive glossy magazines for her, a couple of new books she had mentioned that she would like to read, and a selection of carefully chosen fresh fruit.

He was cosseting her dreadfully and she, fool that she was, instead of insisting on his leaving, was allowing him to do so, outwardly denying what she knew inwardly to be the truth: that she was secretly saving up every tiny memory, that no matter how foolish it might be she hadn't been able to stop loving him at all, that in fact...

That in fact her love for him was actually growing stronger, deepening, widening, until it was beginning to encompass every facet of her life.

'Yes, I still intend to sell,' she agreed, and then gave a tiny sigh. 'That means I'm going to have to go up into the attic and sort out all that stuff up there.'

'Stuff... what stuff?' Luke asked sharply.

'I don't know. Boxes of papers; all sorts of things. The solicitor told me that Mr Burrows hoarded everything and that all the documents and papers they found after his death were collected together and stored away in the attic. Since they had no instructions as to what they ought to do with them, they left them there for me. I just haven't been able to bring myself to touch them.' She gave him an uncertain look. 'I suppose morally, since he was your second cousin, if they belong to anyone then they belong to you.'

'In that case, would you mind if I took a look up there?' He smiled grimly at her. 'Don't worry.

I'm not expecting to find a new will revoking his bequest to you.'

It was still a very sore subject and now Melanie flushed uncomfortably and said stiffly, 'It never occurred to me that you were.'

Only last night he had pleaded with her, 'Just give me another chance, Mel. I promise you, you won't regret it.'

'Take you on trust, you mean?' she had demanded bitterly and had seen the hope, the passion, die out of his eyes to be replaced by a flat despair.

She *wanted* to do as he suggested: ached to do so, in fact, but the trauma of her life prevented her from doing so. There was still buried somewhere deep inside her the illogical childhood belief that for some reason her parents, in dying, had deliberately chosen to desert her.

As an adult she knew that that was not the case; knew that their deaths had been accidental; knew that it was not their fault that she was left alone; but that feeling, that fear of being betrayed, of being rejected, was still there.

Perhaps the fault was hers in that she demanded too much; needed too much.

She started to tremble, moving agitatedly in her chair. No matter how much she protested to Luke that there was really no need for him to stay, he refused to leave her, and didn't she, not so very deep inside her heart, really want him to stay?

'So, you've no objection to my going up into the attic and having a look round?' Luke asked her.

She shrugged her shoulders. 'None at all.'

'I'm not going to give up, you know,' he told her softly.

She looked at him and flushed. 'Luke...'

'You know what I'm talking about. I'm not giving up on us, Melanie. I love you. I want to marry you.'

If he heard her betraying indrawn breath, he didn't show it.

'And I don't care *what* it takes or how *long* it takes. Somehow I'm going to find a way of convincing you that we could have something good together, something worthwhile, something very rare and special.'

'No, Luke,' she told him despairingly, standing up. 'It just wouldn't work.'

She attempted to turn her back on him and walk away, but her sore leg had gone stiff while she'd been sitting down and she half stumbled so that he reached out and caught hold of her, bringing her breathtakingly close to his body.

She couldn't help it—her glance was automatically drawn to his face, his eyes, his mouth. She drew a shuddering breath of air and closed her eyes.

'Melanie, Melanie. I love you so much.'

She knew he was going to kiss her and protested thickly, 'No, Luke, please don't.'

But it was already too late. Already his mouth was on hers. She could sense that he was trying to restrain himself, to rein in his passion. She could even feel him trembling as he drew her into his body.

She tried to resist him, to resist herself, but it was impossible.

As he kissed her, he moulded her scalp with his hands, buried his fingers in her hair, whispered her name over and over again between kisses, telling her how much he loved her, how much he wanted her, how much he needed her.

When he finally released her, Melanie was trembling so hard that she could barely stand up.

'Luke, I can't stand any more of this,' she told him shakily. 'No matter how much you say you love me, I can't forget, can't believe. I can't *trust* you, Luke,' she told him flatly. 'I can't trust you to always be there for me, and I need that; perhaps I need it more than I should. I don't know. I only know that because of the way I lost my parents, because of having to grow up so alone, I have this need in me——'

'I think I know what you're trying to say,' he interrupted her gently. 'And believe me, Melanie, you *can* trust me.'

She gave him a sad smile.

'I wish I could, Luke—believe you, I mean. Oh, and by the way I think I really can manage on my own now, you know——'

'You mean, you want me to leave?' he interrupted flatly.

She couldn't look at him, but neither could she endure any more of this present torture, wanting him, loving him. It would be easier to cope with her feelings if he wasn't constantly there with her, reminding her, weakening her.

'Yes. Yes, I do.'

There was a long pause and then he said quietly, 'All right. I'll go. Will tomorrow be soon enough?'

Tomorrow... Her heart clenched with pain and fear. She couldn't let him go... she couldn't.

'Yes,' she whispered back. 'Tomorrow will be fine.'

While he was looking after her Luke had insisted on taking on all the domestic chores so that she could rest, and after he had cleared away from their meal he asked her if she would mind if he went upstairs into the attic.

'If I'm leaving tomorrow,' he added huskily.

'Yes . . . yes . . . you go ahead.'

He seemed to be gone for a long time. It was quiet downstairs without him. Quiet and very, very lonely. A long shiver went through her. This was what the rest of her life was going to be like. Was she really doing the right thing, or was she simply being a coward, punishing them both because she did not have the courage to take a risk . . . to take him on trust?

Trust . . . that was what it all came down to in the end. She believed she could not trust Luke because he had misjudged her. But he had misjudged her when he hadn't known her . . . when she'd been a stranger to him, and yet wasn't she now equally guilty of misjudging him, and with much less reason?

As she tried not to listen to the urgings of her heart, she wondered what on earth Luke had found in the attic to occupy him for so long.

So long. He had been away from her for less than three hours and she was behaving as though it were a lifetime. How would she react when she really was forced to endure a lifetime, her own lifetime, without him?

While she was still trying to come to terms with the magnitude of that loneliness she heard Luke coming downstairs.

He almost burst into the sitting-room, and rushed over to her, carrying a heavy file of papers.

'I've got something to tell you,' he announced. 'Something that's probably going to give you a bit of a shock.'

Melanie stared at him. It had happened after all. He had found another will. Well, she had half expected it all along, had always felt as though somehow, somewhere, there had been a mistake.

'Well I suppose it's only fair, really,' she interrupted him dully. 'At least I haven't touched the money...or at least not much of it.'

'To hell with the money,' Luke told her. 'And, for God's sake, will you please try to forget this obsession you seem to have that I'm looking for some way to overset John's will? In point of fact, if anyone has a legal right to do any such over-setting that person would be you,' he added gently.

Melanie stared at him, thoroughly perplexed.

'Me? What on earth...?'

She was still seated in the armchair, and now Luke put down the file of papers and dropped down beside her, kneeling on the floor as he reached out and took hold of both her hands in his.

'Melanie, there's no easy way of telling you this. I suppose I should have thought of it earlier, especially knowing John's obsession with the family, but it simply never occurred to me, and...I hardly knew James. He was still at school when I was born, and he went straight from there into the army. I suppose I must have seen him when he came home on leave, but I don't have any memories of having done so, and of course after their quarrel John would never allow his name to be mentioned. Later, when he'd told us that James was dead, Mother told me that he removed every photograph, every single one of James's possessions, every single thing that could have reminded him of James and forbade anyone to ever mention his name again——'

'James? Who are you talking about?' Melanie interrupted him in confusion.

'James, my darling love, was John's son.' He paused, and then, gripping her hands tightly, looked straight into her eyes and said softly, 'And your father.'

It took her several seconds to absorb what he was saying, and when she did, she denied it instinctively, shaking her head and saying, 'But that's impossible. My father's name was Thomas...Thomas Foden. It's there on my birth certificate, my parents' marriage certificate.' Her face crumpled. 'On the death certificate.'

'Yes. Yes, I know. But I promise you that James Burrows was your father. It's all here in this file.

'Listen, and I'll try to explain it as simply as I can.

'Your father James was, according to what my mother told me, a shy, quiet boy. He wanted to become a teacher, but his father was utterly opposed to his having such a career. He wanted his son to go into the army. In those days, national service was still compulsory. Your father must have been one of the last set of young men to have been obliged to undergo it. Quite what happened while he was in the army I don't know. My mother may have more knowledge of the details. All I do know is that as soon as his time in the army was at an end James told his father that he was leaving to train as a teacher. John was furious with him. He wanted James to make a career for himself in the army.

'James told him that this was impossible, that even if he wanted to do so, which he didn't, the army wouldn't have him. There was a terrible quarrel. John lost his temper—when did he ever not? He told James that unless he stayed on in the army he would no longer consider him to be his son. James had always been a gentle, quiet type. I suspect that John had tended to bully him, and fully expected him to give way and stay on in the army. What, I suspect, he had not bargained on was James simply disappearing, simply walking out of this house and never coming back.

'While it's always been common knowledge in the family that James disappeared and later died, what none of us ever knew was what I've found in three papers. Quite simply, once he had left here James changed his name. Quite why he picked the name Thomas Foden I have no idea. There certainly isn't any family connection, but John obviously knew. Not initially—these papers show that it took him a long time to trace James, and that when he had done so it was already too late: James—your father—was dead.'

Melanie could scarcely take it all in. She could only stare at Luke with anguished eyes and ask painfully, 'But if he knew all the time that I was his granddaughter, why did he...?'

'Never acknowledge it . . . never get in touch with you . . . allow you to be brought up by strangers?' He shook his head. 'My darling, I don't know. He was a very strange man; a very lonely man; a very stubborn man; a man full of pride and bitterness.' A sad smile touched his mouth. 'Perhaps we've both inherited more of those family traits than is good for us.' He touched her face fleetingly.

'I can't give you all the answers, Melanie. I suspect most of them have died with John. All I *can* tell you is that you are most definitely his grandchild, and that this is undoubtedly why he made you his beneficiary.'

'But after ignoring me for all those years . . .'

She was crying now, cleansing, healing tears, not of bitterness or misery, but of sadness, not for herself but for the man who had lived out his life so lonely and so bitterly, as she herself could so easily do, as she herself had been going to force herself to do. She breathed in sharply, causing Luke to stand up and take hold of her, lifting her up in his arms and taking her place in the chair, cradling her against him, as he whispered, 'I'm sorry, I'm sorry . . . I shouldn't have broken it to you like that . . . I should have waited.'

'No. I'm not crying for myself,' she told him truthfully. 'I'm crying for him, my grandfather. Oh, Luke, he must have been so alone . . . so unhappy . . .' She gave a final shudder and whispered hesitantly, 'Luke . . . would you please hold me? Close . . . closer.'

'What's wrong?' he murmured anxiously against her hair as he felt her body shudder.

'Nothing . . . not any more. I was just thinking, realising—*I* could have ended up like him, like Mr . . . like my grandfather.'

She felt his body tense against hers, and then he said huskily, '*Could* have? Does that mean . . . ?'

'It means that you're right. That I do love you, and that that love is worth taking a risk for,' she told him passionately.

She felt the tension in the breath he expelled.

'You won't be taking any risk,' he assured her unsteadily. 'I'd *never* let you take any risk, just as I'd never do anything to hurt you. Whatever else you can believe in, my love, you can believe in this: I shall always be there for you, no matter what. Always.'

His lips were so close to her own that she couldn't resist reaching out and touching them, first with her fingertips and then with her mouth, shyly exploring their male contours until he growled softly in his throat and opened his mouth against hers, kissing her with such fierce intensity that she could only cling to him, trembling with need and love.

'So . . . no more doubts,' he demanded when he had stopped kissing her.

'No more doubts,' Melanie responded truthfully. He saw the shadow that crossed her face and told her, only mock teasingly,

'And if you think for one moment that I'm going to let go of you until you've promised to marry me . . . !'

Melanie laughed and teased back. 'If you think for one moment that I'm *not* going to marry you . . . !'

'Then why were you frowning?'

'I was just thinking about this place; wishing I hadn't been so precipitate. I suppose it's sentimental of me, but I'd have liked to have kept it. When we have children...'

'Ah. Now, I'm afraid, *I* have a confession to make: I'm buying the cottage.'

He saw her face and shook her gently.

'Listen to me. Do you really think I could let anyone else live here, sleep here in the room where I first kissed you, first made love to you?' He shook his head. 'No, I was determined that if I couldn't have you then at least I'd have this place and its memories... its echo of you.'

'Well, there's no need for you to buy it now.'

'Yes, there is—the money,' he reminded her softly. 'The money John left you, the money from the sale of this place. Do you still want to donate it to charity?'

Melanie looked at him. 'I thought he'd been so alone, so impoverished emotionally, I thought...' She flushed a little and then looked defiantly at him as she told him, 'I thought it might somehow——'

'Balance out the scales a little,' he said gently for her. 'I know why you wanted to do it, my darling. I was wondering; perhaps in memory of your own father... There are so many youngsters who leave home for one reason or another, only to find themselves alone and beset by all manner of difficulties... Perhaps a charity that aids them?'

'Yes, Melanie agree sombrely. 'Yes, I'd like that.'

'Well, what do you think of the use they've made of your generosity?'

'*Your* generosity,' Melanie corrected her husband as she turned in the passenger seat of his car to take one last look at the building they had just left.

It was a brand new, purpose-built shelter on the outskirts of Manchester, and John Burrows's money—the money that she and Luke had jointly decided to donate to this particular organisation—had been used to furnish one of the dormitories with simple sturdy beds and to equip the shelter with bathrooms and a kitchen.

'I think we've done the right thing,' Melanie responded to him, and then added, 'Those poor children, and they *are* still children, most of them. You know, I used to think the worst thing that could happen to any child was that it was orphaned, but it isn't: the worst thing that can happen to a child is that it has parents who can't or won't love it as it needs to be loved. Those children . . .'

'Many things happen in life that can't be blamed on anyone, parent or child. People suffer pressures under hardships——'

'But nothing like that will ever happen to our child,' Melanie told him fiercely, her hand going instinctively to the small bump beneath her jacket.

'No . . . because along with love we'll give it respect and, I hope, enough freedom and acceptance to allow it to develop as an individual and not as an extension of ourselves. We won't repeat the mistakes of the past, Melanie.'

'No,' she agreed softly, and she knew that he spoke the truth, just as she knew how much he loved her. But now she didn't need that knowledge as a prop or a crutch. Luke's love had set her free to be a whole person in her own right, to go out into the world with confidence and joy, without fearing that she was somehow going to lose him.

Luke had taught her with patience and with love to come to terms with the past, to accept it and to live with it. As she had just said to him, there were far, far worse things in life than being an orphan.

And now she had Luke and Luke's love, and the promise of Luke's child. She smiled secretly to herself. The first of several children, she hoped. Luke was already making plans to transfer the running of his business from London up to Cheshire so that they could make the cottage their permanent home. With the planning permission to extend the floor space, which they had applied for, there would be room for half a dozen children. Her smile broadened.

'What's that smile for?' Luke asked her with husbandly suspicion.

'Nothing,' Melanie told him serenely. 'Nothing at all.'

HARLEQUIN PRESENTS®

A Year DOWN UNDER

In 1993, Harlequin Presents celebrates the land down under. In March, let us take you to Northland, New Zealand, in THE GOLDEN MASK by Robyn Donald, Harlequin Presents #1537.

Eden has convinced herself that Blade Hammond won't give her a second look. The grueling demands of trying to keep the sheep station running have left her neither the money nor the time to spend on pampering herself. Besides, Blade still considers her a child who needs protecting. Can Eden show him that she's really a woman who needs his love . . . ?

Share the adventure—and the romance— of A Year Down Under!

Available this month in
A YEAR DOWN UNDER

NO GENTLE SEDUCTION
by Helen Bianchin
Harlequin Presents #1527
Wherever Harlequin books are sold.

YDUF

Where do you find hot Texas nights, smooth Texas charm and dangerously sexy cowboys?

DEEP IN THE HEART

Wedding Bells—Texas Style!

Even a Boston blue blood needs a Texas education. Ranch owner J. T. McKinney is handsome, strong, opinionated and totally charming. And he is determined to marry beautiful Bostonian Cynthia Page. However, the couple soon discovers a Texas cattleman's idea of marriage differs greatly from a New England career woman's!

CRYSTAL CREEK reverberates with the exciting rhythm of Texas. Each story features the rugged individuals who live and love in the Lone Star State. And each one ends with the same invitation...

Y'ALL COME BACK...REAL SOON!

Don't miss *DEEP IN THE HEART* by Barbara Kaye. Available in March wherever Harlequin books are sold.

HARLEQUIN®

my Valentine

1993

The most romantic day of the year is here! Escape into the exquisite world of love with MY VALENTINE 1993. What better way to celebrate Valentine's Day than with this very romantic, sensuous collection of four original short stories, written by some of Harlequin's most popular authors.

**ANNE STUART
JUDITH ARNOLD
ANNE McALLISTER
LINDA RANDALL WISDOM**

**THIS VALENTINE'S DAY, DISCOVER ROMANCE
WITH MY VALENTINE 1993**

Available in February wherever Harlequin Books are sold.   VAL93

ROMANCE IS A YEARLONG EVENT!

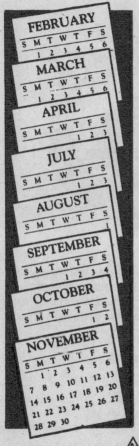

Celebrate the most romantic day of the year with MY VALENTINE! (February)

CRYSTAL CREEK
When you come for a visit Texas-style, you won't want to leave! (March)

Celebrate the joy, excitement and adjustment that comes with being JUST MARRIED! (April)

Go back in time and discover the West as it was meant to be... UNTAMED—Maverick Hearts! (July)

LINGERING SHADOWS
New York Times bestselling author Penny Jordan brings you her latest blockbuster. Don't miss it! (August)

BACK BY POPULAR DEMAND!!!
Calloway Corners, involving stories of four sisters coping with family, business and romance! (September)

FRIENDS, FAMILIES, LOVERS
Join us for these heartwarming love stories that evoke memories of family and friends. (October)

Capture the magic and romance of Christmas past with HARLEQUIN HISTORICAL CHRISTMAS STORIES! (November)

WATCH FOR FURTHER DETAILS IN ALL HARLEQUIN BOOKS!

CALEND